unnerving

twelve unsettling stories plus one

BLUE FORGE PRESS

Port Orchard ✹ Washington

Unnerving Toxic
Twelve Unsettling Stories Plus One
Copyright 2025
by Blue Forge Press

Cover art by Siobhan Merrow
Interior art and design by Siobhan Merrow

First Print Edition August 2025
First eBook Edition August 2025

ISBN 979-8-89439-054-3

For information about film, reprint or other subsidiary rights, contact: blueforgegroup@gmail.com

This is a work of fiction. Names, characters, locations, and all other story elements are the product of the authors' imaginations and are used fictitiously. Any resemblance to actual persons, living or dead, or other elements in real life, is purely coincidental.

Blue Forge Press is the print division of the volunteer-run, federal 501(c)3 nonprofit, Blue Legacy (EIN 83-4307421), founded in 1989 and dedicated to supporting artisans marginalized due to race, age, disability, economics or other factors. We strive to empower storytellers from all walks of life with our four divisions: Blue Forge Press, Blue Forge Films, Blue Forge Gaming, and Blue Forge Sound. Find out more at www.BlueForgeGroup.org

Blue Forge Press
7419 Ebbert Drive Southeast
Port Orchard, Washington 98367
blueforgepress@gmail.com
360-550-2071 ph.txt

To the truths we learn
in the darkness
and in the long midnights
of our discontent

CONTENT WARNING

This book is intended for mature audiences as these stories are purposefully meant to unsettle the reader. If one month's story is too intense, skip that month. While the editor and Blue Forge Press have selected and edited each of these stories, ultimately you are responsible for curating what you read.

For a full list of triggers by story, please write to:
blueforgepress@gmail.com

table of contents

TOXICC

JANUARY

Jason and Julie's Last Date

Jennifer DiMarco

I exhaled phantoms into the cold night air and wondered if winter would ever end. There was nothing quite so unpleasant as Brooklyn in January; and to think it was unseasonably warm at forty-two degrees!

The restaurant had screwed up our reservation (or I had) and we'd had to wait half an hour. Then the food was unremarkable because their award-winning chef had been accidentally deported and the waiter was distracted and kept cutting you off. You'd left the table three times, excusing yourself politely, but you must have been upset. Once, I even thought you went back to the kitchen! No surprise, our food was served soon after. I didn't want to leave a tip but you'd have none of that; it was twenty percent even if the service was crap.

Despite it all, you were composed—grateful, even—quiet and mindful and demure. As always. I grinned a little and snuck a look at you now. My darling girl. Never rattled. Never raised your voice. Careful and collected. I wouldn't change a thing about you.

Well, maybe one thing.

"You aren't cold, Julie?"

You didn't respond at first. You were looking out over the dark river, lost in private thoughts. This was who you were. Whether gardening in your roof-top greenhouse, developing your own photos, or electroplating intricate metal sculptures, you were artistic, driven by your internal world, forever contemplating.

Cars crossed the bridge above us, making streaks of light beyond your beautiful profile. You were an image from a Soho gallery, your backdrop a study in urban architecture and ropes of light but your face so collected, so Renaissance; a strawberries and cream complexion haloed by cherubic auburn curls. The pert bow of your lips and slight up-turn of your button nose made you look younger than you were; eternally caught in an ageless place that made people describe you as 'sweet' and 'cute.'

I was so lucky to have you.

An ardent gust of wind sliced through my jacket as if I were nude. It caught me off guard and I made a sound; that's when you turned. You blinked at me once, twice, and a shadow of confusion crossed your face. As if it had never occurred to you that sitting outside in the dead of winter might be chilly. Your eyes were glacial blue in the riverside lamplight. Your face was incredibly still.

"Where are you?" I asked, all the love I felt for you in my voice. All the admiration and captivation. By nature, you were introspective and insightful. I'd had two years of watching you drift deep into thought and I never ceased to be amazed by your contemplations when you chose to share them. Were you pondering Yang-Mills existence and mass gap? Bounded rationality versus loss aversion? Whether or not to bake cinnamon rolls on Sunday? You were remarkable—a Julie of all trades.

I never knew what to expect.

You just looked at me. Then you looked at all of me. Your eyes slid off my face and down over my bundled body, huddled beside you on the bench, my hands shoved deep in my pockets, my thighs clamped together like a last bastion of defense between winter and my balls. I mean, I wanted kids *some* day.

"What are you thinking about, love?" Sometimes you needed me to ask twice. Sometimes it took you an extra moment to return to the here-and-now from wherever your brilliant brain took you. Sometimes, you still didn't answer. But tonight you did.

"I was thinking about a boy named Jason."

I grinned at you and cocked an eyebrow. I played up the flattery and touched my heavily insulated chest in mock surprise. "*Moi?*"

You said: "Not you."

Oh. You weren't being coy then. My hand returned to my pocket.

You were still looking at me. No. You looked *past* me. You looked into the night, into your own memories.

"A boy I went to elementary school with."

Scrambling to regain my cool, I offered, "Twenty years ago. Wow. What, uh, made you think of him?"

"Twenty-five," you corrected me then you turned away to look back over the tumbling, ink-black river.

Did you sound... irritated?

The wind shifted and traffic sounds increased. I fought the impulse to shudder, to shake my whole body as if to shake off a layer of frost. "Maybe we should—"

"He was always cold, too." Disgusted.

I stopped breathing. For a just a moment I was too stunned to move. Your tone was unmistakable but also impossible. You would never…. You had never even once… with anyone, about anything—

You answered as if just now hearing my questions: "There was a group of us. Smart kids. We walked home together. Five of us. Good number. Jason was second to last on the route. Penultimate."

When you spoke, your breath barely clouded the air. It was as if you were as cold inside as the night around us. You were perfectly at ease and I felt increasingly uneasy.

"My house was last so we had time together, just the two of us, every day." Your eyes narrowed a little. Concentrating. Trying to remember some fine detail. "It was after Christmas break, early in January, like now. Our fifth grade year."

Your back was straight, your shoulders squared in your open wool coat over your russet cable knit sweater. Your small hands held the front of the bench on either side of your skirt. You sat perched on the edge.

"There was a wooded lot. Probably half a lot, really, because no one could build there. Through the bare trees we—me and Jason—spotted a shed. Maybe an old utility shed from when the city brought power to the Projects. The windows were cracked and the door hung off one hinge. There were rats." You lifted your chin into the cold wind. "It was perfect."

I looked out over the river now, too. I pictured what you spun. Saw the lot of skeleton trees. Saw the shed. I imagined you and I, children together, standing in curiosity on a winter's day.

"'That's my shed,' I told him. 'My daddy bought it for me to be my clubhouse. But he doesn't have the time to fix it up yet.'"

I looked back at you. You continued to look into the

night, into the past.

"It was all a lie," you confessed immediately, easily, and without any hint of regret or shame. "The shed was condemned. I'd taken down the yellow flyer myself."

I felt something behind me and whipped my head around to look. Nothing was there. Just the park, a few distant couples and solo walkers, clusters of dormant trees in silhouette. I looked back at you; you hadn't noticed my alarm. The fine hairs on the back of my neck were like small needles of paranoia down my frigid spine.

"He offered to fix the shed for me," you told me. "I knew he would. For months, I'd purposefully asked for his help in class. Had made a point of praising him when we made birdhouses for the community garden. I'd planned everything perfectly, even timed exactly which day to point out the shed. Friday." You nodded faintly, agreeing with yourself twenty-five years later. "He'd have the whole weekend."

"Wasn't that dangerous?" The question slipped out. I was cold and unsettled but mostly I just didn't believe that my mild-mannered girlfriend had once manipulated another kid into doing a bunch of work for her.

You turned your head to look at me as if in slow motion. I actually had time to think: *Why is she moving so slowly?* Your face was expressionless. Still as a frozen lake. Then your eye twitched. A hard pull that snagged a sneer.

"That's my point," you snarled, suddenly low and seething.

I straightened, ram-rod. You kept staring at me.

"*I would have been named Jason.*" You said it like it explained everything. "If I'd been born a boy. And he was the first person I knew with that name." You didn't blink. "*My* name."

"But—"

You were looking right at me but didn't hear me.

"I was ten years old in fifth grade. Just ten years old. And already I knew he had things I would never have. Just by being born *him* instead of *me*." Somehow, your eyes burned blue as propane. "I hated him so much. I was so jealous. He'd *stolen* from me. Like a thief."

I exhaled a billow of vapor as if just remembering I needed to breathe. The wind took the cloud and tore it apart, ripping it past you. You looked at me with your burning eyes in your frozen face and I couldn't find the words.

You continued: "It collapsed. The shed. The floor gave out along one side and the whole thing caved in. No one found him until Tuesday night. They asked us at school on Monday, careful not to alarm us but wondering if anyone knew or had seen anything. Where could he be? The policemen were so tall, I remember that."

"You... were just a kid." My voice wavered, smaller, thinner than usual. What were you telling me?

"It was entirely premeditated." You're so clear, concise, utterly unapologetic. "He couldn't just have what was meant to be mine."

You turned yet again to the black river. Your intensity diverted, I felt relief so deeply it scared me. My heart was pounding, my breath fast and shallow.

"Julie...?" I said your name as if calling to you. As if trying to conjure you, the you I knew, from the depths of this person beside me now. This person I did not know... and did not *want* to know.

"I've always known," you told me. "I've always known why I did it. And it's never bothered me. It still makes perfect sense."

You slid back, letting go of the edge of the seat. You continued to watch the river but now your body blended into the angles of the bench, the cold steel and your cold bones in harmony.

You told me, "I don't like to be threatened."

My mouth opened but only silent confusion emerged.

You turned just your head. "There can only be one of me."

I had never doubted it. My hands laid in my lap. When had I taken them from my pockets? My fingers were blue to the first knuckles.

You looked down at them. "It usually doesn't take this long."

Your tone was so mild, not even curious but almost bored. You tucked yourself against me, covering my hands with your own. Your grip was surprisingly strong.

"Jason." A statement, then another: "It's a preservation thing." So obvious. Painfully obvious and entirely too late. "You understand, don't you?"

But I could tell from your tone that you don't care. You're didn't even try to. I couldn't seem to catch my breath as though the air itself was devoid of oxygen. The night swam in splotches of shadow as thick as blood.

"I've always known what's right and wrong," you told me casually, resting your cheek on my shoulder, your breath cold against my neck, my pulse racing, skipping, slowing. "It's just who I am."

FEBRUARY

sweethearts

Joe Nasta

EAT ME

"Eat me," bold black letters outside the paper box declared. "The one you desire will come," the instructions read in cursive. The top opened like a cigarette packet. Europa shook it gently until a single green heart-shaped candy landed in the center of her palm. In red, the same message appeared in coated sugar.

"Eat me." She bit into the chalky sweet. The candy fell apart in crumbles on her tongue before dissolving sublingually. The sickly taste lingered on her lips a moment longer, then the feeling hit.

Pupils widened. Heart picked up a half pulse extra every few seconds. Strength coursed down the muscles in her legs. Clarity and calm overtook her entire body.

This feeling must be love, she thought.

For months, she'd been wrung with yearning. The ache twisted through her chest and abdomen for hours at a time while racing thoughts too quick to comprehend coherently shocked her brainstem. This feeling was an unbridled desire, but it had no object. Her lust coursed up and down her ribs, through her hips and pelvic floor, and down her glutes and hamstrings but the throbbing want had no place to escape, no willing wound to meet hers and receive the offering of breath, blood, passion, and other bodily fluids, no mutual opening that would pour back into her the same care, hunger, passion that would replenish her.

In the throes of another sleepless night, her want led her out of bed and her one-bedroom apartment, onto 15th Avenue at 3 am, and past Uncle Ike's Weed Dispensary. The eerie night was empty but the flashing lights of the storefront sign cast moving shadows as if something scurried just out of view. The chilly air reached through her hoodie zipper, shocking her breast, and through the seams of her plaid pajama pants—the only thing she had left from her last boyfriend.

A new neon sign she'd never noticed before beckoned. An arrow. It pulsed pink and yellow, irresistible. Has this alley always been here? She'd lived on Capitol Hill for a year but maybe she could have missed it... In any case, she was drawn in. More arrows appeared as she entered deeper into the corridor, leading to a dead end. A red cabinet, a metal mallet on a chain, fragile glass. Her ache.

"Break me." It shattered so easily. A few shards landed on her forearms, microtearing the skin so bright red burst forward under the pulsing light. Nothing but the box of conversation hearts inside.

The one she desired. The shadow in her periphery.

With a gulp, Europa swallowed.

FLIRT

The shadow darted out of the alley down a street lined with mansions. Europa was pulled forward by the new energy that continued to grow within her and followed without question.

Coyly, the shadow allowed her to catch glimpses during the chase. The shadow sped faster and she began losing her breath matching it. They weaved across the deserted street and down the sidewalks together, almost levitating.

Next to a well-manicured hedge, its shape widened; she was chasing a bull. The excitement of discovery inflated her chest as her pulse quickened, adrenaline searing the back of her neck. The bull shifted from a mere shadow to a softly radiant spirit, growing more light each time it allowed her to see him.

The street ended at the entrance to Volunteer Park. A path emerged between the European Birch trees, who weeped joyful green leaf-tears to greet her as they stooped their bark-spines to look her in the eyes.

As they passed the threshold together, the bull began glowing brightly and his white light gave Europa power and strength—she threw her head back and laughed, overwhelmed with renewed excitement as her beloved guided her along the dirt pathways towards the center of the park, his beckoning bright more constant than before.

BE MINE

The bull was gone. The grey amphitheater was filled with darkness. The wide lawn held only dead, yellow grass. The air softened around her into a putty as Europa's excitement sunk into her bones, suddenly heavy.

However, this was not the familiar longing she knew. This feeling was despair. Her movements became sluggish as she fell to the ground, skinning her knees. How could she have lost her beloved so easily after their brief communion?

She buried her face in the dirt, banged her fists on the solid damp earth. A growl emerged from her stomach, up her chest, out of her mouth. The hunger.

BESTIE

The grief worked itself out of her body and she was weightless again, suddenly floating five feet above the ground. The bull stood in the center of the amphitheater's stage, watching her. The relief tumbled from her lungs into a smile, bringing a shriek of delight.

A red blanket appeared with a picnic basket filled with sustenance—artisanal cheeses and meats, a baguette, a bottle of wine. The bull watched her savor each morsel.

Pungent smell of the cheese delighted her while the hardened texture of the bread made her chew. The gentle fizz of her wine washed it down. Grateful for her dear friend who gave her this care, she allowed the meal to fill her as she floated further off the ground.

A beam of light reached from him to her. They were connected without touch and beyond expectation. They basked in the tender glow of being together.

GIGGLE

On the outer edges of the field, murmurs and rustling. They were being watched. Europa felt infinite sets of eyes observe her landing softly on her feet.

The cold night hit her again, exhilarating. Above, the moon and stars. The bull reared onto his back legs, dissipating the beam of glow connecting them.

The spirits watching them laughed with glee.

There was no embarrassment. Instead, she was filled with the warmth of being witnessed, celebrated.

The bull raced away from the amphitheater. She followed, the train of spirits bubbling behind.

HEART THROB

The two of them reached the door to the tower.
A drum beat.
The spiral staircase.
Around them, water.
She floated.
Echoing sound.
The bull's horns grew.
Europa allowed herself.
Suspend.
The spirits' giggles turned to booming belly laughs.

At the top she could see above the trees in all directions.

She laid back, arms dangling and she rose again into the air.

Bang.

This was the feeling.

The bull made her feel safe.

Then the water entered her mouth.

CALL ME

Opened eyes. Where was she? Count to ten. Hospital bed. IV drip. A steady beep on the heartbeat monitor. Movement rustling out in the hall.

Europa had no memory past a dark night, cold metal on her chest, a burst of neon, and a saccharine flavor on her tongue. Grogginess still made the room a bit blurry, but she could turn her head in the direction of a nurse entering the room.

"What happened?" she asked, clearing her throat and tenderly sitting up. A few blinks of her eyes cleared her vision enough to focus. She felt calm and empty. Coming to her senses, she realized the ache she'd been plagued with for months was gone. This feeling was secure, embraced, grounded.

"We believe you've been hallucinating. Your blood tests show traces of a new drug called Pothos. It causes severe delusions and a sense of euphoria. They found you face down at the top of the water tower in Volunteer Park."

When they discharged her, she put on her hoodie and flannel pajamas. A plastic bag contained her personal effects: her wallet and cellphone, a leaf, a cheese rind, and an almost-empty container of candy hearts. She removed each one to put into her pocket, pausing with the paper box in her hand.

Under the fluorescent glow bouncing off the gleaming linoleum, the packet was easier to examine than in the dark night. There was a phone number printed on the bottom and one final sugary heart inside. "Call me," the yellow candy read.

She popped it into her mouth and picked up the phone.

MARCH

the job created

Gregor Fjellrev

Specialized Predictive-Interference—Submodel RAL, Module 99134/125000 initializing...

Date logged as 07/09/2051, 0100 Hours

Confirm Primary Purpose: "Scan online traffic and profiles for individuals potentially hazardous to the current social order, generate and implement methods by which they may be eliminated without accountability." As set by Secretary Travis Glovebill on 06/29/2051.

Primary Purpose Loop confirmed, beginning search...

FLAG: ORANGE-5 SUBTYPE DELTA

Subject: Norman X. Dechaineaux

Location: Ypres, Belgium, EU

Subject Personal Hardship Level: 3.6/9

Brief for Superiors: Subject Norman Dechaineaux is an unemployed male student of twenty-nine years of age. He is a student of engineering [and] art.[F1] Electronic sales traffic and bank records suggest living on single sales of intricately painted artwork approximately three months at a time. Critically well-received, though not mainstream. Quote "admirably blends the precision of math and engineering with a [free-flow]^{F2} abstract style that can be appreciated both up close and from afar."

Subject was unable to complete degree course for art but has attained Associate's degree in engineering, and continues further [education.]^{F3} Initial analysis of lifestyle confirms subject ability to balance work and study, note [high resourcefulness.]^{F4}

[Subject family social class noted as lower-middle with a 17% margin of error, subject personal social class noted as middle with a 8% margin of error.]^{F5} Private data access authorized by fifth flag status.

Accessing voting history...

Accessing medical records...

Accessing personal accounts...

Confirming potential social upheaval potential...

Subject PSUP Rating: 77—High risk of advocating for social reform. Medium-Low risk of personally enacting social reform. Medium risk of general participation in social upheaval.

Generating SPIRAL Protocol model...

SPIRAL Protocol: Begin by blocking sales of artwork online by accessing art sale website moderation team account and enacting Shadowban Procedure on subject Norman Dechaineaux's entries to said website(s) with waxing intensity, beginning at 10% suppression, increasing weekly until 100% Shadowban is achieved. Subsequent e-sales drain will lead subject to pivoting towards in-person sales. Generate no less than sixty artificial profiles as art patrons to clog email and text channels with bogus offers that go nowhere, staggered one after the other over no less than two weeks at a time each. If possible, have these profiles suggest meeting at noted local cafe for no-show procedure. Subject will likely purchase food at such meetings and enact subsequent gradual financial drain. Monitor all legitimate traffic to subject entries on sites and employ Lagspike Procedure in the event legitimate users attempt to make contact for potential sale.

SPIRAL Stage 2: Assess subject Norman Dechaineaux's state after three months of commercial isolation and no-show non-patrons. Generate artificial appointment traffic at local medical offices as needed to prevent being seen for physical or mental assistance. Generate additional artificial profiles with less convincing realism after initial profiles have been expended. Within two months of stage 2 initialization, subject will no longer believe any outreach as legitimate, and self-isolation will begin. During this or previous stage, use local assets to enact minor sabotage on subject's vehicle to incur financial toll if possible.

SPIRAL Stage 3: Maintain appointment traffic at any medical facilities subject devices search for. Continue artificial patron generation and Shadowban Procedures on all relevant platforms. Adjust subject primary device advertisement algorithm to gravitate towards sporting goods stores. Gravitation procedure should be adjusted to an extended period of time considering subject intelligence and resourcefulness.

In the unlikely event subject Normal Dechaineaux begins to suspect program efficiency, purchase one or two pieces of artwork from online store to distract (LoH Protocol.)

SPIRAL Stage 4: Financial toll likelihood to force

subject to drop out of studies calculated at 92% at this stage. Otherwise, continue Shadowban procedures as well as baiting to local cafe for no-show meets until this point or until self-termination is confirmed. After drop out is confirmed, adjust primary device advertisement algorithm towards knives and bladed instruments, as well as climbing gear, directing to website designation KRN-BG.

SPIRAL Stage 5: Inject Bricking Program into primary device through embedded malware on website designation KRN-BG if present. If subject affords new equipment, enact consistent excess of bad packets to hinder device performance by at least 27%.

SPIRAL Conclusion: Subject will become financially destitute, to the point of suicide or self-isolation to the point of being effectively neutralized.

FLAG REFERENCES

F1: See supporting document "Maintaining separation between STEM and Humanities for population and cultural control (DDSCI-39)"

F2: See supporting document "Flagged adjectives for subjects of interest (DDCON-03)"

F3: See supporting document "Regulating Education Access (DDCON-05)"

F4: See supporting document "Flagged adjectives for subjects of interest (DDPSY-03)"

F5: See supporting document "Dangers of permitting upward mobility (DDSOC-01)"

Module 99134 generation of SPIRAL analysis and protocol elapsed generation time 1.552 seconds

WARNING: SUBJECT OUTSIDE DEFINED OPERATIONAL AREA BY OVER 3,500 MILES. LOG WEEKLY OOA REPORT NUMBER 8,676

Bypass accepted, override code Red Sixteen Theta confirmed. Logging weekly Red Sixteen Theta authorization instance number 8,676. Executing SPIRAL protocol initiation on subject Norman Deschaineaux. Modules 44, 621, 5960, 9945, 20175, 50467, 124044, have not yet returned daily SPIRAL candidate. Assisting Module 44.

FLAG: RED-7 SUBTYPE OMICRON
Subject: Brian Thomas O'Donnell
Location: St. Paul, Minnesota, US
Subject Personal Hardship level: 4.9/9
Brief for Superiors: Subject Brian Thomas O'Donnell is a male factory worker of nineteen years of age. He is currently employed as an Overnight Alarm Monkey. Bank records suggests ability to live comfortably on current salary, spending most spare time [writing][F1] and playing grand strategy video games. Social media presence notes [high levels of dissent][F2] and a strong desire to [leave the US][F3] for Europe. Accessed bank statements predict that at current net value, spending habits, income, and intent to attend [European college,][F4] financial ability to reliably leave the country permanently will be achieved in approximately nine years. [Subject holds a *Shodan*, or first-degree black belt in Karate][F5] and access of attending Dojo's computers place subject's test for *Nidan*, second-degree in nine months.

Subject currently lives at parent's house. [Built-in

camera on subject's primary device returning black screen, suggesting covering][F6] with 99.99% certainty. Secondary device detected identified as Samuel Thomas O'Donnell personal computer with uncovered camera. Access suggests office, [bookshelf noted with several notable titles][F7] (see attached image.)

Private data access authorized by Red-type initial flagging.

Accessing voting history...

Accessing medical records...

Accessing personal accounts...

Confirming potential social upheaval potential...

Subject PSUP Rating: 132—Low risk of advocating* for social reform. High risk of enacting social reform. Extremely high risk of general participation in social upheaval.

Generating SPIRAL protocol model...

SPIRAL Protocol: Begin by accessing experimental neural network implant of local delivery driver (PART ID TCN-2,) remote-inject software worm for overheat. Local traffic will coincide with resulting fatal crash of delivery vehicle into the personal vehicle of Master Toichi Ideki. Dojo subject Brian O'Donnell attends will close within six months of incident after loss of leadership.

SPIRAL Stage 2: Monitor subject Brian O'Donnell's involvement with investigation and legal regarding incident (lawsuits against delivery company for overworking deceased driver, lawsuits against experimental implant manufacturer, lawsuits against surgical firm that implanted said implant, criminal charges against all aforementioned companies.) Adjust subject personal device advertisement algorithm, heightening martial arts supplies prevalence and adding attorney ads, alongside static banners for firearms. Adjust news delivery algorithm to personal device as necessary to invoke appropriate level of investment into investigations and trials (i.e., heightened numbers of articles on the incident, and similar neural network implant overheat incidents) before proceeding to stage 3.

SPIRAL Stage 3: Adjust judicial assignment of cases to ensure each criminal and civil case regarding the incident is assigned to judge identified as Deschuan Melagra, a shareholder in the company that designed the neural network implant. Bribe as necessary to ensure all parties accused are neither liable nor guilty in the deaths of either the delivery driver or Master Toichi. Bribe higher-level officials as necessary in the event of appeals to ensure rejection. Monitor any purchases made by subject Brian O'Donnell.

SPIRAL Stage 4: Upon subject acquisition of any firearm or heightened number of bladed weapons, generate social media post containing the personal address of judge Deschuan Melagra. Adjust algorithms as necessary to ensure subject Brian O'Donnell finds and interacts with said post. Permit street justice to take its course.

SPIRAL Conclusion: Subject Brian O'Donnell will be killed in police encounter following the assassination. Death of corrupt judge will simultaneously serve as paltry pacification for locals, and subject Brian O'Donnell will be honored, but not martyred by the greater peasantry population. General public moving on will fully take place within six months of subject death with 82% certainty, 99.99% certainty within twelve months.

FLAG REFERENCES:

F1: See supporting document "Flagged hobbies and professions for subjects of interest (DDCON-02)"

F2: See supporting document "Flagged adjectives for subjects of interest (DDCON-03)"

F3: See supporting document "Citizens leaving Equals Profit lost: On the importance of stifling savings and keeping them in! (DDFIN-02)"

F4: See supporting document "Importance of keeping education domestic (DDSOC-06)"

F5: See supporting document "Flagged hobbies and professions for subjects of interest (DDCON-02)"

F6: See supporting document "Flagged habits and traits for subjects of interest (DDCON-04)"

F7: See supporting document "Flagged literature for subjects of interest (DDCON-05)"

*- Module notes that 'low risk of advocating' is not a product of an actual low risk of assisting in social reform, but rather that instead of advocating, subject is far more likely to instead take a much more active role in bringing forth social reform disruptive to current order.

Module 99134 assisting Module 44 generation of SPIRAL candidate and protocol elapsed time 3.121 seconds. Module 44 logged 7.096 seconds of search before assistance. Executing SPIRAL protocol initiation on subject Brian Thomas O'Donnell. Module 5960 has not returned daily SPIRAL candidate. Assisting Module 5960.

FLAG: BLUE-3 SUBTYPE BETA
Subject: Lt. Cmdr. Ryan Kastor, USN

Location: USS Minnesota (SSN-783), at sea. Coordinates classified.

Subject Personal Hardship Level: 4.0/9

Brief for Superiors: Lt. Cmdr. Ryan Kastor is currently serving as an Acoustic Warfare Analyst aboard the USS Minnesota. Subject's military record shows repeated instances of turning down promotions that would carry transfers to Ohio-Class submarines, demonstrating [strong preference towards the Virginia-Class.][F1] Subject's commanding officers have noted [exceptional resourcefulness][F2] in tactical training, 'Able to make a lot happen with a little' quoted from Capt. Michael Beauregard. Noted incident during basic training with US Army National Guard in which during mil-sim wargaming, subject, as squad leader, noted that rival team had already deployed within the fenced field of operation, and responded by leading his squad around the fence of the field and striking rival team from behind their own lines. Drill instructors at the time noted that subject Ryan Kastor had chosen to ['counter-cheat,'][F3] in his own words, 'I have no problems fighting fair, but I also have no problems throwing sand in the face of someone who kicked me in the crotch.' Kastor would later transfer to Navy OCS after short part-time career in Army National Guard.

Private data access authorized by existence as government employee.

Accessing voting history...

Accessing medical records...

Accessing personal accounts...

Confirming potential social upheaval potential...

Subject PSUP Rating: 82—Medium risk of advocating for social reform. Extremely high risk of enacting social reform.* Low risk of general participation in social upheaval.

Generating SPIRAL Protocol model...

SPIRAL Protocol: Begin by injecting malware code into data stream of next uplink with SSN-783 once the vessel surfaces for regular data download of orders and updates. Malware will cause submarine's navigation systems to subtly return unreliable data on surface weather and oceanic current paths, as well as undersea terrain.

SPIRAL Conclusion: Between the subtle points of unreliable, human error will ensure the vessel, and all hands, are lost. SSN-783 will be perpetually listed as 'on patrol' when she fails to return to port, per naval tradition.

FLAG REFERENCES:

F1: See supporting document "Who will survive the dropping of the bombs, and where they will be (DDMIL-04)"

F2: See supporting document "Flagged adjectives for subjects of interest (DDCON-03)"

F3: See supporting document "A special kind of honor: How to spot diamond officers in the rough (DDMIL-03)"

*- Module notes that subject is exceptionally likely to enter a career in politics after retiring from military service, and will be extremely effective in enacting social reform. Likelihood of achieving US Senate seat near certain. Likelihood of achieving state governor office exceptionally likely. Likelihood of achieving US presidency above average.

Module 99134 assisting Module 5960 generation of SPIRAL candidate and protocol elapsed time 8.015 seconds. Module 5960 logged 14.992 seconds of search before assistance.

WARNING: SPIRAL PROTOCOL INITIALIZATION WILL RESULT IN MASS NON-TARGET CASUALTY INCIDENT. LOG WEEKLY MNTC REPORT NUMBER 3. SPIRAL PROTOCOL INITIALIZATION WILL RESULT IN EXTREME LOSS OF GOVERNMENT PROPERTY. LOG MONTHLY LGP REPORT NUMBER 1.

Bypass accepted, override code Red Sixteen Theta confirmed. Logging weekly Red Sixteen Theta authorization instance number 8,680. Executing SPIRAL protocol initiation on subject Ryan Kastor.

All modules report successful generation of daily SPIRAL candidate, analysis, and execution of protocol. Specialized Predictive-Interference—Submodel RAL, Module 99134/125000 powering down for day at 0101 hours.

APRIL

the Chicken or the Egg

Michelle Lee

I slapped my hand over my phone as the morning alarm ripped me out of a tranquil sleep, its cartoonish melody mocking me, and swiped my fingers over the silence button without even opening my eyes. The room was chilled, the early spring morning filtering through my open windows. I could hear the rain over the low purr of my rotating fan, which was only ever off when the power went out. Five days a week, this routine hardly varied. My life was rather predictable.

My eyes still closed, I swung my protesting body into a sitting position, my legs dangling off the side of my mattress. They didn't reach the floor because the mattress was high. It sounded better than saying I was short. I stretched all my muscles, trying to prepare them for the movement that was about to thrust them into the start of the day. Getting old wasn't for the weak.

I slid down until my feet touched the floor and finally cracked open my eyes to witness the dark of night slowly fading to gray, which would probably persist throughout the day because of the rainy April weather. I was okay with it since spring was one of my most challenging seasons with the rising pollen counts. The rain kept it down to tolerable, and the proper medication assisted the efforts.

I trudged to the bathroom because gravity pressed on my full bladder, making that my first morning priority. After that, I brushed my teeth, blindly grabbed whatever clean clothes were hanging in the closet, and dressed. It was Monday, my husband was out of town, and I still had to go to work after a weekend full of chores and very little fun or relaxation.

I had hoped that with Miller gone, I would have had some peaceful downtime. Instead, my brain decided it would be an excellent time to clean since I couldn't sit still or figure out what else to do with myself. Now I got to go to work where I would have to sit and listen to Hildy for five days in a row and concentrate all my efforts on not choking her to death as she discussed her favorite topic of conversation—herself.

Hildy was an energy vampire. If you were anywhere near her for an extended period, you know, longer than five minutes, the energy drained out of you, and suddenly you were exhausted. My theory is that it took all efforts not to duct tape and staple her mouth closed. If it wasn't a conversation about whatever new miracle drug that was going to make her lose all her weight, it was talking about her fiancée who was seventeen years younger than her, and his sudden reluctance to get married, which then made her dive into every single one of his faults. Those of us who worked on a rotation and had to be in her vicinity tended to call out sick at least once.

It was my week to be near her. I would be assisting a senior biochemical medical doctor specializing in genome manipulation. He was hoping to be able to find a cure for dementia using stem cells from different animals. Working as an assistant wasn't glorified, but it could be interesting depending on the doctor paired with you. Dr. Samuels was brilliant and loved talking through what he was doing and the results he sought as he worked. It was a great working experience when I paired with him. I learned things I never hoped to understand.

Hildy was the receptionist for the small company. Since we didn't get many people coming in from outside, she sat at a desk in front of one of the open areas where many research assistants worked beside their doctors. Dr. Samuels also favored this area because it was so open. I secretly thought he wanted to be out here to see whatever asinine thing would come out of Hildy's mouth. He once told me she would make a great test subject, making me laugh uncontrollably.

When I arrived at work, I settled my stuff into my assigned locker, locked my stuff inside, and pocketed the key. I grabbed safety goggles and a lab coat and jammed some gloves and hair nets into the pockets. I wasn't sure if we were researching today or doing lab work, and I liked to prepare for either. I slid my arms into the lab coat and buttoned the front of it.

There was an hour and a half until Hildy showed up, so I hoped to capitalize on the quiet. I retrieved Dr. Samuels's notebooks, work laptop, and the pens he used and got everything situated. I rushed out of the room to make a cup of coffee for him, which wasn't a part of my job, but I liked having his expected setup ready for when he walked in the door, which would be in four minutes. Dr. Samuels was punctual and regimented but without the attitude typically associated with those personality traits.

He was a jokester, had a fantastic sense of humor, and loved to poke innocent fun at people. For one of the top people in the company, he was one of us.

"Good morning, Mirabelle," Dr. Samuels said as he fell into step beside me. "Is that for me?" He gestured to the steaming up of coffee. "How much time do we have before the dragon descends?"

I snickered at his nickname for Hildy. "About an hour and a half," I told him, handing him the cup of coffee. I watched with a small smile as he inhaled the scent and closed his eyes. He'd once told me that he didn't have coffee at home or he would drink it all day and night long. He'd become a caffeine monster, never sleep, and become the company freak. It was too bad he didn't involve himself in personnel matters, or Hildy would no longer be an issue.

"Well, let's take advantage of the quiet and spend some time out here gathering research, and then we'll spend some time in the lab. Ultimately, we'll finish the day out here because I'm trying to put together the data and hoping it forms a bigger picture before we actually try to create the formula and put it to the test on live subjects," Dr. Samuels explained.

"Do you want me to grab the file with the scans?" I asked. "I only took the research notebooks and your laptop this morning."

"No, it's okay. I have the digital scans on the computer. I'll need a folder from Dr. Fong. The one that she is working on regarding anti-aging in animals. It's a bullshit project that I disagree with, but she's made progress in slowing the aging process in chickens to gain more production time out of their lifespan. I think she's narrowed in on something that might correlate to what I am doing," Dr. Samuels relayed while we walked.

"Isn't that the double project for the farming commission and a beauty company?" I wondered aloud.

"That's the one. I wouldn't say I like dabbling to change the DNA of a creature for our gain. However, the flip side is that is what I am doing with my research precisely," Dr. Samuels hypothesized.

"I wouldn't say that. Curing dementia is saving people's lives. Creating a serum to erase wrinkles or tighten skin isn't the same thing," I defended him. "Messing with chicken DNA so they live longer to produce more eggs is a gray area. Regardless, I'll grab the file for you. She won't need it since she's off today."

"Okay, see you in the pen," Dr. Samuels said, walking away from me, his long strides eating up the distance.

I went down the hallway and veered off toward the offices. The rule was that none of your research left the facility. I wasn't worried that I couldn't find Dr. Fong's notes. I was concerned that the results were exaggerated because of office gossip I'd heard sometime last week. Of course, I needed to consider the source, Hildy. You could tell her that it was raining outside, and the next thing you hear is that the rain had raised the water level in the dam to dangerous levels, and we were all in danger of the dam bursting and drowning. All the while knowing there wasn't a dam near us.

I grabbed the file from Dr. Fong's cabinet and was almost out of the office when another assistant walked in and bumped into me. I'd dropped the file in the accident and bent over to pick it up while apologizing for not watching where I was going.

"Is that the ant-aging file?" Lori asked me. "I was hoping to use some of the research for Dr. Kronenberg."

"Yeah," I told Lori. "Dr. Samuels needed it, too."

"Here, I'll make a copy of what I need, and you can take it," Lori offered, holding out her hand for the file.

I shrugged and handed it over. I didn't know what Dr. Kronenberg was working on at the moment, and if he needed it too, who was I to argue? Lori made a copy of only two pages and returned it to me. She warned me that Hildy had shown up early and was making the rounds telling everyone about her latest argument with her boy toy. I rolled my eyes in response.

"I suspect she's also going to add in every bite of everything she ate over the weekend and each piece of clothing she's wearing and will tell us all how much each piece cost and where she got it from," I added, already feeling the energy getting sucked from my body.

Hildy was forty-seven and the guy she was dating was almost thirty-one. I figured he needed a mommy role filled in his life. Hildy was short, round, and had more junk in her trunk than someone living in their car. Her face was splotchy with red acne patches, and she'd recently colored her hair darker to make herself look younger. It didn't work. Makeup, false eyelashes, diet pills, and stiletto heels wouldn't make her more desirable. It was her personality that was repellant.

I wasn't a beauty queen and wasn't trying to impress anyone. My husband was ten years older than me. I was two years older than Hildy and looked ten years younger than her. I stopped that train of thought because I didn't want to get sucked into a mental comparison of me versus her. I wasn't in competition with her and she didn't deserve space in my head. I had work to do.

o you see that spot right there?" Dr. Samuels asked me, tapping on his screen.

I popped my head over to look at what he was pointing to. There was a white spot in the scan where there shouldn't be. "Is it dust?" I asked stupidly.

Dr. Samuels laughed. "That's what I thought it was at first, and I'm surprised I didn't notice it earlier. Look at this scan from a week ago." Dr. Samuels switched his screen to show both scans, which showed the spot wasn't on the other scan. "Still could be dust, right?"

I nodded because I didn't know. For this reason, I liked working with Dr. Samuels so much. The knowledge I gained was valuable, if mostly irrelevant, to my job. Sometimes, the other doctors asked me if I saw the same thing they did, and once, I could point out something else that I had learned from Dr. Samuels. I'd ridden a confidence high that day. I watched as Dr. Samuels put a third image on his screen.

"It could be, but on this scan, the spot is still there, only a smidge larger," I pointed out. "Could there be an issue with the CT scan? Maybe we need to schedule maintenance on the machine."

"Could be," Dr. Samuels nodded admirably at me. "However, I suspect this spot is where dementia forms. The chemical Dr. Fong injects to slow the aging process triggers this spot's growth. It looks like she has stumbled on a chemical cause of dementia. It's only a hypothesis at this point, but something in the brain is reacting to the chemical she is using. Dementia shrinks your brain, to put it plainly, and usually starts in the region of the brain right here."

"To the clean lab we go?" I guessed, knowing how Dr. Samuels worked.

"I don't think we need the clean room yet, but yes, to the lab." Dr. Samuels pulled some pages from the file of scribbles of chemical compounds I would never understand and then grabbed one of his similar pages. "Bring your notebook. I'll probably give you some things to research for me as I run a couple of experiments on some brain samples I have. On second thought, we'll go to the clean room."

Are you with Dr. Samuels all week?" I turned to see my work child standing behind me. She loved to remind me that I was older than her mother by two years and two days.

"Yeah," I confirmed. "We borrowed Dr. Fong's research yesterday. I put the file back before I left last night."

"It's not there." Janey shook her head at me. "That's what I came to find you about. She told me that Dr. Samuels was sharing with her."

Janey was tall and reed-thin, with dark hair and fair skin. She was a natural beauty with an easygoing, fun attitude until you pushed one of her buttons. Her laugh was infectious and it was a joy to be around her. Even when she was mad, I liked being around her.

"He left before me yesterday and I put it back." I thought about our movements before Dr. Samuels left and what I did to close our day. "I know I put it back because I stopped outside Dr. Fong's office and talked with Cora. Dr. Samuels isn't here yet, so I know he didn't grab it. I don't think he would anyway since I made a copy of the research page he is still working with."

"Oh, I didn't think you had it," Janey corrected me. "I was going to ask if you knew anyone else working on something similar."

"Lori made a copy of some pages yesterday," I remembered. "But then she gave it back to me."

"Dr. Fong is pissed," Janey whispered to me. "I've never seen her like that, and that tiny woman is scary."

Dr. Fong was typically docile, always rushed, and preoccupied with her research as she ran from one place to another. She had a soft-spoken voice, didn't make it past five feet tall, and had an ageless beauty that made you think she was a shy twelve-year-old. Angry wasn't an emotion in her wheelhouse.

"What aren't you telling me?" I crossed my arms and leaned against the wall, giving Janey a raised eyebrow look.

"She thinks someone on the team is trying to poach her formula," Janey confided. "She wants me to request a copy of the security footage from yesterday to this morning when she got here. It sounds paranoid to me, but she's worried that if it's not someone here, then someone from the cosmetics industry broke in and stole her research."

I let go of my breath in a controlled exhale. That was quite the claim. Dr. Fong wasn't prone to paranoia or known for flinging accusations out about her team. It could be nothing more complicated than simply misplacing the file by someone who borrowed it. I didn't want to think some cutthroat cosmetic company was breaking into our secure building to steal an untested formula for anti-aging.

"I'll ask Dr. Samuels if he can send an email asking if anyone has it," I suggested calmly. "Maybe someone borrowed it after I left and forgot to put it back."

"Maybe." Janey shrugged. "But Dr. Fong is about to lose her mind. She keeps saying it's an unproven hypothesis and too dangerous to test."

"That's true for most of our research here," I

countered. "Okay. I'll go see if Dr. Samuels is here yet."

Janey and I parted ways, and I headed for Dr. Samuels's office when the lead assistant, Lizette, found me. Her face pinched with worry and her strides were long and fast. This morning didn't look too promising for a relaxed and productive day at the office.

"No Dr. Samuels yet?" Lizette asked me as she approached.

I shook my head and then shrugged. "I was just going to see if he was in his office. What's wrong?"

"His door is closed. I wasn't sure if that meant he wasn't here or if he was in the lab already," Lizette told me, alarm in her voice. "Unauthorized lab use after hours last night is what is wrong." Lizette waved the missing research papers for Dr. Fong in my face.

"Where did you find those?" I asked. "Dr. Fong is going to stroke out because she can't find them. Janey said she was angry. At least that mystery is solved."

That caused Lizette to pause for a moment. "Fong is never angry; that doesn't sound right. Come with me to find her. We can talk on the way."

I sped up to keep pace with the determined woman. "What are we talking about?"

"I found these papers in the lab," Lizette waved the papers again. "There were also printouts from someone searching what these formulas were. By that, I mean, like a translation of the written-out formula to an ingredient," Lizette explained.

"What?" I asked, confused.

"You know, like H_2O is water. Someone did that for all the compounds in this formula. It appears they tried to make it. I've had to call in a crew to clean the lab because the air had a taste to it and Geiger counters were making noise. It's like a Chernobyl reenactment in there," Lizette fumed.

"Our lab is a hazmat zone?" I stopped in my tracks and stared at Lizette as if she were a lifeform from another planet. "Are you sure? Radioactive?" I blurted out.

"Girl, I'm sure. I'm waiting for a text to see if we need to lock the building down. The lab door was open. So whatever toxic shit happened in that lab, the air out here isn't clean either. That means we are all here until medically cleared," Lizette growled angrily.

"Why aren't we in safety gear?!" I screeched. The implications were far worse than I initially thought.

"Because I just found out five minutes ago, and we have no idea what we are dealing with, and the CEO hasn't responded to her messages yet." Lizette poked at me. "You don't think I'm freaking out? I need someone with a level head to help me get this straightened out. We find Chen and explain what happened, and if she says we need to gear up to be safe, that's what we do. Whatever is in the air, we've already breathed it in."

"Don't wait for the CEO. Lock the building down." I shoved Lizette. "Make the call. We'll deal with the fallout later. We have to do it if we can keep anyone else from putting themselves in danger."

Lizette stopped before Dr. Samuels's office and gave me a sad look. "If we are wrong, we could be in serious trouble. It could mean our jobs."

"If we are right, we are helping," I countered. "Do it."

Lizette entered Dr. Samuels's office and turned on the emergency system, which automatically locked the building down, turned on the red emergency lights, activated the encapsulated decontamination room, and reversed the airflow. To the best of my knowledge, this was the first time someone had used the system.

We stood around fully decked out in our safety hazmat gear while Dr. Samuels and Dr. Fong huddled around her desk, having a semi-quiet conversation. Unfortunately, Dr. Samuels had entered the building before Lizette triggered the alarm. I hoped Dr. Samuels would be spared and be outside pulling strings to get us all cleared as quickly as possible.

The company had a hazmat team cleaning the safe room next to the decontamination room so we could gather after doing rounds in the cleaning chamber. The small blessing in the entire situation was that we hadn't gotten actively trapped in a hazardous building with the toxic Hildy. I would have gladly licked the surfaces of the building clean if she had been present. I wasn't the only one to feel that way, either. Several people had commented about the good luck of her being late as usual. The hazmat suit was punishment enough.

It was impossible to have a private conversation while dressed in the containment suit, so most of us sat around and pretended not to listen to Dr. Samuels and Dr. Fong discuss what could have happened in that lab and who could have been the culprit. The CEO had the security footage pulled, and the doctors huddled together to watch who had entered the lab.

The Hazmat team had collected all our electronics and they were undergoing a cleaning process that wouldn't harm them. We couldn't even call our family to tell them what was happening. Upon entering the safe room, the cleaning team returned them to us while they decontaminated the rest of the building. It was like we were on a movie set for a film about a deadly disease released into the air to wipe out the planet.

Except this was our reality, not something I could turn off and return to whatever chore I should be doing. I knew Janey felt as detached as I did as if we were watching from outside our bodies, even as we stepped into the decontamination chamber together. We said nothing, followed the automated directions piped through the speakers and watched each other go through the motions. We all trained for it, though we never expected it to happen.

When we came out and put on clean scrubs, we sat in the clean room against the wall in the corner and breathed in the sterilized air. The process took a couple of hours to get all the personnel through and another five hours to declare the building safe. It was only after an intense debate with authorities on keeping us overnight with Dr. Samuels battling for our freedom that we were allowed to leave and go home for the day with a stern warning to watch for any symptoms of illness and to report them immediately. The center would be closed tomorrow.

Every person walking out of that building had a look to them that stood my hair on end. Haunted, detached, exhausted, drooping shoulders, head hung down, and sunken, bruised eyes. It was something I'd see in my dreams later.

I'd forgotten to turn my alarm off after I returned home and so bright and early, I was awake. I'd finally spoken to my husband and told him everything that had happened. He was rightfully upset and worried and it wasn't long after I was up that I started getting several texts asking if I felt okay. Two were from Miller, and I had one from Janey,

Lizette, Dr. Samuels, and Cora.

Before responding, I returned to the bathroom, dug through a drawer to find my thermometer, and took my temperature. The reading was slightly elevated but not considered a fever. I responded to each with the temperature and then stated that I had no other symptoms other than fatigue. And the exhaustion could be easily explained by yesterday's activities. I saw no reason to be worried.

That didn't mean I wouldn't lie down and take it easy on my unscheduled day off. I settled on the couch with a blanket, turned on the TV, set the volume down super low, and grabbed my book to read. I don't know when I dozed off or how long I was out. When I woke up, my body ached fiercely, and some reaction was evident. I slowly reached for my phone and called Lizette.

"Hey," I greeted when she answered. "Something is happening," I croaked. My voice was thunderous in my ears and my sense of smell was potent. "I smell like soup."

"Girl, stop." Lizette laughed weakly. "Something is happening to me, too. My arms look like raw chicken skin, for real. I texted Dr. Samuels my symptoms; he's got an entire list of everything everyone is experiencing. He said almost everyone in the building who was there had something going on. The building is going to remain closed for another couple of days. He wants people to have time to recover or fully develop whatever the symptoms are."

"Did you say chicken skin?" I rasped. My brain felt like it was moving through tar, but something niggled at the back of my mind. "The research we were working on from those papers you touched used chicken DNA. Dr. Samuels was trying to tap into how dementia ate away at the brain and something in the chicken genome resisted."

"Are you telling me I am going to turn into chicken?" Lizette screeched as much as her voice would allow. "That's not acceptable."

"It's not what I'm saying," I replied, fumbling around for an explanation that made sense. "Maybe this is all temporary, and we'll be okay and get back to ourselves in a few days. It could be our body reacting to something within the chicken genome. I don't know. I'm not a doctor. I can only relate back to what that research was about."

"This is unreal," Lizette sighed. "I refuse to be a damn bird. Text Dr. Samuels your symptoms so he can add them to his list," she instructed me. "Stay in touch. I need to boil myself in a bath and see if I turn into soup."

The theory was far-fetched, though I had to admit that I didn't know enough about DNA, genomes, and other such things to see whether it was possible or not. Turning a human into a chicken seemed more like science fiction than fact. Yet, I couldn't rule it out either.

I texted Dr. Samuels about my odd symptoms and then added my wonder about the connection I drew to chickens. It was a risk worth taking, even if he thought I was an idiot and inhaled more toxic air than I should have.

I tried to break it down to what facts I knew. Dr. Samuels was working on two projects using DNA strands from chicken. Dr. Fong was working on two projects using the same research, though possibly different DNA strands than Dr. Samuels—one for an anti-aging beauty serum. Someone got into the lab, used the research already done, and tried to create the formula, but now everyone in the building was sick somehow. Maybe my mind was making leaps that it shouldn't. I didn't have as much information as I thought I did, and I wasn't a doctor who understood the nuances of the symptoms the way Dr. Samuels did.

A few minutes later, I received a text back from Dr. Samuels asking if the odor was when I sweat or all the time. Then came another text that said he agreed with my assessment that the coincidences of chicken-like symptoms were too hard to ignore. A third text dinged my phone seconds later that said he was doing active research for a way to remedy the situation but was having a hard time since he didn't know what was in the serum. He wasn't even sure if the symptoms people were having were permanent or temporary.

It was frightening to think these symptoms or changes would be permanent. On a whim, I texted Janey to see how she was faring, and then I called my husband to fill him in, but he didn't answer. I texted him and asked him to call when he had time.

The following message I received was a company text declaring the facility closed for the next two days. I wasn't surprised, but I did hope they would pay us. Easter wasn't far away; some of us had people to feed and groceries to buy. A half of a week without pay wouldn't be good.

I wandered over to the kitchen to take stock of what food I had on hand and what I would need to cook a small Easter dinner. I couldn't help noticing that my eyesight was far sharper than usual and that I could hear the sounds of cars on the street. In fact, I could hear electricity humming throughout the house. I grabbed a pad of paper from my junk drawer and wrote down everything I noticed that was different.

I flipped the page and wrote a list of groceries I would need for Easter dinner. Nothing had to do with chickens unless you counted the colored plastic eggs. Deciding to take a bath to ease my muscle aches, I went to the bathroom and wondered if I would be the chicken in a tub of hot water to make soup.

by the time our two forced days off were almost over, most everyone was feeling better and had only a few lingering side effects. Mine was the super sharp hearing. I could live with that. If it got overwhelming, I could use earplugs to dampen the noise. I'd rather have that than walking around smelling like chicken soup.

Lizette sent out a group text suggesting an Easter-themed potluck for Friday to lighten the mood and atmosphere. Dr. Samuels was the first to respond and said he'd bring a ham. The rest of the crew responded after that and soon the food list was enormous. I was happy Lizette was organizing this feast and not me. I replied that I'd bring cookies and Lizette sent me a text asking me to make snickerdoodles. That was easy enough to do.

I'd spoken to my husband and filled him in on everything. He was understandably upset and told me he would be home by Friday when I got home from work. It was earlier than he'd planned to be home, which made me happy.

I made my dough early and would chill it in the fridge until Thursday night. That way, I would be bringing freshly baked cookies for Friday. I made a double batch to leave here for my husband to find when he got home. It also added the benefit of having the house smell like freshly baked cookies instead of any lingering chicken soup smell.

After that, I finished my chores and laundry, read a book, and watched television before bed. Thursday came, and I was ready to be back at work. I dressed in a brightly colored pair of scrubs and had a fleeting thought that I looked like an Easter egg, but I didn't care enough to change.

The first thing I noticed when I pulled into the parking lot at work was that Hildy was already there. My spirits sank and I struggled to regain them before I entered the door. We all started before she did and as happy as I was to be back at work after our scare, I wasn't ready to deal with the constant stream of talk about everything Hildy.

"Suck it up, buttercup," I told myself as I parked. I reluctantly got out of the car, wondering what I would be walking into, yet I kept putting one foot in front of the other. The need to see if my coworkers were okay was more substantial than my urge to avoid Hildy.

The astringent chemical smell of the industrial cleaners used in the facility still hung in the air as I pulled open the front door after using my keycard to unlock it. I heard the lock engage after the heavy door swung shut behind me. Hildy wasn't at her desk, so I scurried down the hallway to stash my stuff in my locker.

I saw signs of Easter along the way and suspected it was Hildy putting colored eggs in random places with the fake plastic grass under them. Oddly enough, I also spotted a few feathers and didn't stop to think too much about it. I didn't want to get cornered and stuck in a conversation with her, so I kept my head down and went about my business.

I saw Janey decked out in full-coverage protective wear in the locker room. I didn't blame her for wanting to be safe, and I couldn't lie or say that the thought hadn't crossed my mind either. I don't think anyone wanted to experience a repeat of the lockdown. However, I wanted to believe that Dr. Samuels wouldn't allow us back in the facility if it weren't safe.

Lizette walked in as I locked my locker and pocketed my key. She glanced at Janey, who was texting and hadn't noticed us yet. I searched Lizette for any signs of chicken skin and anything else that might relate to what we experienced, but I didn't see anything other than her paleness.

"How do you feel?" I asked her quietly. I still didn't know where Hildy was and didn't want my voice to carry in case she was there.

"Better, but not like myself," Lizette answered as she stowed her purse in the locker and grabbed a clean lab coat. "What about you?"

"I don't smell like soup anymore, but my hearing is so acute I swear I can hear dust move in the air," I replied with a wry smile. "I'll take that over the soup thing."

Lizette pulled up her sleeve and showed me the bumpy skin. "This is a lot better, and it only happened to my arms. This patch looks like goosebumps, like I'm cold. It's a thousand times better than it was. I hope it continues to improve and isn't permanent."

"Did you come into contact with any of the spillage?" I asked, sitting on the bench.

"I don't think so, but I can't be sure," Lizette answered as she sat beside me. "There might have been some on the pages I picked up. I kept replaying it in my mind and was in panic mode, so I don't know if I was as careful as I should have been."

"Scary," I murmured as I heard the sound of clicking heels. Click-clop as the heel struck the ground, and her foot slapped the pavement. "I hear Hildy."

"Damn!" Lizette bolted to her feet. "Janey! Let's go!" Lizette called out. "Unless you want to talk to Hildy."

"No, I don't." Janey snapped her head around to us and quickly joined us at the door to the hallway. "What if she's out there?"

I listened to see if I could determine how far away the steps were from us. I guessed this sharpened hearing thing could be a benefit. "It sounds like Hildy's to the left of us, not in this hallway yet." *Click-clop, click-clop,* the steps were slow. "Maybe she's still putting eggs everywhere."

Janey's face wrinkled up. "Those are real eggs; I hope they don't stink up the place."

"Worry about it later," Lizette grumbled. "Let's go to the desks to see who else is here. Safety in numbers and all that."

Our soft-soled sneakers barely made a whisper of sound as we walked, though my ears still picked it up. It sounded padded with a little whoosh as our pace was rapid to avoid encountering Hildy. We rounded the corner and Janey peeked her head around the doorway.

"Clear," she declared. "What's with the random feathers? That's not Easter. Bunnies are easter."

I heard the click-clop getting closer and shoved the girls into the room. "She's behind us," I warned.

Lizette and Janey snapped into action, and we hurried as a trio to two other assistants standing in the corner talking. Cora looked at us as we approached, and the other gal, Sofia, stopped talking. Neither of them appeared to have any lingering side effects, though they gave Janey a fearful look because she was covered from head to toe.

"Are you sick?" Cora asked Janey when we stopped near them.

"No, but I don't want to catch anything or get exposed again," Janey declared with a little attitude. "I have kids at home and don't want to take any chances."

"Are our assignments still the same?" Sofia asked Lizette.

"Yeah, we will stick to the rotation schedule,"

Lizette said. She glanced back over her shoulder and didn't spot Hildy. "Hildy is coming; that's why we came over here."

"She's putting eggs everywhere," Cora complained. "Isn't that a sanitary issue since it's food? And have you seen her? She's changed."

"What do you mean?" I wondered. "She wasn't even here the day we discovered the breach and contamination."

I guessed I would see for myself since her footsteps were closer now. Lizette, Janey, and I slightly turned our bodies so the doorway was clear. Two seconds later, I heard each of them gasp when Hildy walked through the doorway.

Hildy was what some people used to call big-boned. In the age of labels and things we weren't supposed to say, we now just said big. She had a lot of junk in the trunk, and her legs used to look significantly ballooned. When she walked in, we noticed her legs were incredibly small, and her midsection was quite round. The second thing that drew our eyes was the bunched-up, wrinkly, loose skin around her neck.

"Girl," Lizette breathed out. "What the actual fuck?"

"Is this plastic surgery gone wrong?" Janey asked. "It's been three days; you can't lose weight like that targeted in one area. Not without surgery."

Lizette gave me a wide-eyed stare. I didn't need to say anything; I knew what she was thinking. However, I didn't think Hildy was smart enough to combine the serum. She had absolutely no medical or scientific background. How would she have even read the research?

"No one ever told me what they saw on the security footage," Lizette whispered. I don't think the others could hear her, but my supersonic hearing heard every word.

"Hello, ladies!" Hildy shouted. "Happy almost

Easter! Do you like my new shoes? I just bought them from this website I stumbled across. I did a lot of shopping over our days off. Aren't they great? My fiancée loves them."

The moment it appeared that Hildy aimed herself in our direction, Lizette clapped her hands sharply and declared loudly, "Okay, we have our assignments. Let's get prepared for the day. We've got a lot of work to do." Lizette jammed her elbow into my side as I noticed Hildy's gait differed. It was probably those stupid heels she insisted on wearing.

"Walk with me to get the research papers," Janey said, tugging me after her.

"Where is everyone going?" Hildy called out. "Did you see all the Easter eggs I colored and hid everywhere in the building? I spent a lot of time doing it. Whoever gets the most eggs will get a special prize I made special. We all know I'm kind and generous like that. It'll be fun, I promise. I'm excellent at this stuff!"

No one stopped walking away. However, I noticed that everyone was looking at Hildy with a twisted, odd expression of morbid curiosity. The train wreck we couldn't stop staring at. Every step she took was flat-footed, different than when she came down the hallway. Her head bobbed forward with each footfall.

"Why is she so weird all the time?" Janey whispered before we rounded the corner.

I didn't say anything in case Hildy's hearing was as sharp as mine was. I didn't like her, but I wouldn't go out of my way to hurt her feelings. I motioned for Janey to stop talking and walked faster. I didn't consider us safe until I couldn't hear Hildy's shoes clopping on the concrete floor.

I didn't want to tell Janey my theory about what was happening. It was so wild, and I had no idea what the security cameras showed about who had broken in and caused the incident. What if it wasn't who I suspected? Making false accusations wouldn't help anything and only cause tension in the office.

"Do you think Dr. Samuels will be here today?" Janey wondered as we entered his office to get the research papers. She opened the cabinet and then yanked her hands away. "What if they are still contaminated?" Panic grew in her widening eyes.

"They aren't," I reassured her. "Those are copies freshly printed from paper just opened and put in the machine after everything was clean." It was standard protocol in situations like that. The crew even changed the paper towels and toilet paper in the bathroom. It seemed like a waste but I understood that some things can live on surfaces for an extended period.

"Got them." Janey pushed the file drawer shut and we turned to see Dr. Samuels enter and close the door behind him.

"Sorry, ladies, give me a moment to think. Can one of you grab Lizette and bring her here?" Dr. Samuels asked as he moved around us and dropped into his chair. His face appeared drawn and haggard, like he hadn't slept.

"I'll go," Janey offered, practically leaping around me and scampering down the hall to find Lizette.

"Between us," Dr. Samuels started, "she has almost zero effect from that contamination. If anyone has a chance to survive, it's her."

"You think this is fatal?" I whispered. Terror froze the blood in my veins. I shivered.

"I really don't know," Dr. Samuels replied slowly. "I've been running tests on myself and have seen changes I can't explain. DNA tests take longer, and it's hard to predict until I get results." Dr. Samuels shook his head as if he were arguing with himself. "I can't explain what happened here. I will show you and Lizette some security footage and would like feedback. I also want to draw some blood from Janey."

I blinked a few times to try and gather my thoughts. Seeing Dr. Samuels baffled by anything was a new experience for me. It was only a matter of minutes before Janey was back with Lizette. Janey moved to stand in the corner and Lizette sat in the chair across from the desk.

"Janey, I'd like to draw some of your blood to test against my other samples since you have almost no symptoms of anything. Will that be alright with you?" After Janey nodded, Dr. Samuels continued. "You three are the ones I will trust with this, as you don't gossip." Dr. Samuels swiveled and logged onto his computer, turning the monitor so we all could see the screen. "This is the security footage from the night of the incident. I have it queued to right before the time it happened."

All three of us intently watched the empty hallway. My eyes flickered over to where the time displayed at the bottom corner of the screen and it was well past the time anyone should be in the building.

A few minutes later, a man who appeared to be in his thirties, with facial hair and a hat obscuring his face, walked into the frame. He approached the wall where a motion sensor for a building alarm hung. The man inexplicably reached up and pulled the wires from the sensor, then clapped his hand and wiped them like they were dirty.

"Why disable a motion sensor when the alarm isn't even on?" Lizette wondered.

"That's what I thought, too," Dr. Samuels replied. "But keep watching."

Janey was focused on the guy with a frown on her face as if she were trying to place him from somewhere while Lizette and I watched a blanketed figure enter the frame. It was hard to determine the height from the camera angle, but the man was taller than the lumpy blanket. The shoes, however, gave away that the figure was female unless it was a crossdresser.

"Those shoes," Lizette whispered and trailed off. I knew what she was thinking because we'd both heard the story about the app Hildy bought them from.

"Is there audio?" Janey asked. "I'm guessing that guy thinks he disabled the security camera because of his actions. It looks like he is trying to tell the lumpy blanket they can come out," Janey observed.

"Well, he's dumb," Lizette stated in a matter-of-fact tone.

"Well done, Janey," Dr. Samuels praised her. "That answers that question. Anything else?"

"I think that's Hildy's boyfriend," Janey said slowly. "I'm not one hundred percent sure, but it matches what I can remember of him from the parking lot, and the hat is the same."

"Interesting," I drawled and tapped my finger against my chin. "I know there is more than one pair of those shoes in existence, but what are the odds that it's not her?"

"Slim," Dr. Samuels agreed. "We didn't know who he was, though, and how he fit into this."

Lizette made a humming sound and stared at me. I shrugged because I knew Hildy wasn't smart enough to read those formulas and it was apparent that the guy wasn't the brightest bulb either. Maybe he was one of those guys who fed into a female's insecurities and made them do crazy things to appease them. My gut told me it was Hildy who concocted the plan. Her vanity knew no bounds.

"Well," Janey supplied, "he's way younger than her and she's paranoid about the age gap. You can't seriously tell me that you guys haven't heard her going on and on about it and all the ridiculous crap she does to make herself try to look younger," Janey scoffed.

"Oh, no," Dr. Samuels grinned. "We've all heard and seen it. Repeatedly."

"The fake eyelashes, stilettos, inappropriate clothes, neon makeup, and hair extensions," I droned on.

"But none of that explains how she is even smart enough to understand anything on those papers," Lizette argued. "We work with this stuff daily and struggle to know what it is, even when it comes to Googling things. I mean, I'm not dumb by any means, but I'm not a doctor."

"Sometimes, all it takes is the spark of an idea for the most desperate to think it's a great plan and then fail spectacularly," Dr. Samuels postulated. "Yet, it still happened, and we all suffer from it. While your input confirms my suspicions, it's not hard evidence to take to law enforcement since no clear facial shots identify them."

"What about the cameras in the clean room?" I asked.

"Spray paint." Dr. Samuels sighed. "The only intelligent thing either of them did. I had hoped I could use the footage to see what they used, but unfortunately, we have nothing."

"So we have to wait and see what develops in us and her?" I fumed.

"It's not like you didn't know she was selfish," Janey unhelpfully pointed out.

"I choose to believe that she didn't know this would

happen," Dr. Samuels replied. "I know you three and the others don't care for her. From what I can see, her DNA is changing alarmingly. It's not an effect I believe she expected. Who wants to turn into a chicken?"

"I certainly won't be eating chicken ever again," Lizette chimed in with a wry grin.

"Okay, one last request, ladies," Dr. Samuels said, sitting forward. "Since you are all on the floor, can you keep an eye on Hildy, note any changes you see, and log the date and time you noticed them?"

We all nodded our agreement and moved to leave the office. Dr. Samuels stopped us with a wait motion, and we waited while Janey fought the containment suit so Dr. Samuels could draw some of her blood. Once he completed that, we left the office. I was angry and scared and battled to determine which was more prevalent. I kept returning to Dr. Samuels admitting he didn't know if this was fatal to us.

"I'm not taking this gear off," Janey firmly stated as we returned to the main research area.

"Kinda wishing I would have thought to put it on." Lizette frowned. "Nothing Dr. Samuels said was promising."

"He can't even say if this is fatal or not," I confessed. "It makes me want to choke Hildy."

Janey burst out in laughter, which sounded strange in her gear. "You want to choke the chicken."

Lizette giggled. "That *is* what you said."

Thankful for the laughter, we rounded the corner and didn't see Hildy at her desk. We all shot concerned looks at each other and took our place at our respective desks. Since Dr. Samuels was my partner, I didn't have much to do, and I just prepped the desk for his arrival. Then I heard the clopping sound of feet coming down the hallway. I caught Lizette's eye and motioned to the hall. She understood my meaning without having to say anything.

Hildy came around the corner, her head still bobbing, and she waddled. I swear I saw some feathers sprouting off the side of her neck. I jotted down the date, time, and symptom. Then, I added how she walked, which I noticed this morning.

"Hey, everyone! I made deviled eggs last night and just put them on the breakroom counter. Go eat them!" Hildy crowed like she accomplished a colossal feat.

"Oh, that sounds fantastic," Dr. Fong said excitedly. "That's my favorite part of the Easter holiday." She stood up and left to indulge herself.

Even if I liked deviled eggs, I wouldn't have gone under the circumstances. No one else got up to sample the food and in fact, most people didn't even look up from the work on their desks. That in itself was odd for this group of people. Usually, quiet chatter filled the room as they discussed the research they were working on. Instead, it was as silent as a cemetery. I wasn't sure where that disturbing thought originated, but now the cemetery was stuck in my head.

My cell phone vibrated, and I snuck it out of my pocket to read Lizette's text. *It's like a tomb here, and the groundskeeper is Hildy. Something is wrong.*

Do tombs have groundskeepers? I texted back to Lizette. *But I agree.*

Cora suddenly came out of her stupor and stood up. She scanned the room and, not seeing who she was looking for, sighed heavily and stomped out of the pen and down the hallway. I checked the schedule to see who she was working with and realized that Lori wasn't there. Cora must be working with Dr. Kronenberg today, who was also absent. Actually, now that I looked around, several people were missing. I could have sworn there were more here earlier this morning.

My cell phone vibrated again, this time with a group text from Janey to me and Lizette. *I think you guys should put masks on. Something is happening with the others.*

I wasn't going to second-guess it. I whipped a mask out of my pocket and settled it in place. I glanced over to see Lizette had done the same thing. That was when two other assistants suddenly stood, each with a distant, not quite there look in their eyes, and stomped aggressively out of the room.

"Those three are in the lead on the egg hunt," Hildy gloated with a smirk. "You should collect some, so you don't miss out on the prizes."

My email pinged with a message from Dr. Samuels:

Ladies, there has been a development. I believe the eggs that Hildy placed throughout the facility are noxious. The shells are deteriorating and releasing a gas. Dr. Fong has died after eating the deviled eggs, and I am not doing well after breathing the air. Please take precautions to avoid coming into contact with them. I'm initiating another lockdown in fifteen minutes. This building has a subterranean level with an escape tunnel that lets out about a mile down the road to a small side road that looks like a drainage ditch from the road. You can access it from the decontamination until through a hatch in the floor. It is in the far-right corner from the entrance, and a panel will lift from the floor when you activate the button, which is slightly different from the rest of the floor. I want you three to head in that direction before I initiate lockdown. Alert authorities of a new virus and tell them to access notes on my laptop. If you can, suit up as Janey has done and leave now.

I shot up from my desk and saw the same wild look in Lizette's eyes that I felt in mine. I motioned with my head to the hallway, and we each started to walk casually in that direction, though we all wanted to bolt. Things were happening fast and it was hard to keep up and process.

"We're going to find some eggs!" Janey called over her shoulder to Hildy, who was watching us with beady eyes. That was when we saw a white colored film cross over her eyes and then disappear as if she had some other type of eyelid.

"Oh, good!" Hildy preened in her nasal voice. "Best wishes."

"What the fuck?" Lizette whispered and pulled us out of the room faster.

"There won't be time to change," I whispered back. "It takes a good fifteen minutes to get suited up."

"Are we going to ignore the eyelid thing?" Janey dazedly asked.

"Yes," Lizette and I answered simultaneously and emphatically.

The hallways were eerily quiet until we got close to the breakroom. I heard low guttural moans from inside and I desperately wanted to stop and help, but Lizette shook her head no. I knew we were on a time limit if we had any hope of surviving this. I hadn't even processed the information that Dr. Samuels was resigned to dying in the building along with our coworkers. I hadn't had time to work through anything. It was fight or flight, and we were in flight mode.

We stuck to the middle of the hallway as we walked at a fast clip so we weren't close to where Hildy randomly placed the poison eggs. It didn't stop my skin from burning, though. I wanted to slap at it and scratch, yet I managed to refrain. "Did she lay the eggs?" I wondered out loud.

Lizette let out a hiss and scratched at her forearm. I reached out to stop her and froze with my hand in midair. A greenish-black patch was growing in size, spreading across her skin like an ink stain. I knew without looking that I was experiencing the same thing. The pain was intense, and it felt like someone had flayed my skin open and exposed my nerves to frigid air.

"We have to get out of here!" Janey screamed at us. She yanked on my sleeve and tugged me after her as she ran towards the decontamination room. Lizette was right on my heels, though her breathing was labored.

How did things deteriorate so quickly this morning? What was in those eggs? Thoughts raced through my head as Janey searched the floor for the button to release the hatch. I knew then I wouldn't make it out. Something in my mind told me I would die here, and it wasn't just a fatalistic reaction to everything. I reached painfully into my pocket for my phone and texted my husband, letting him know I loved him and was sorry. I sketched out a brief explanation of what was happening and that we were trying to escape but didn't think Lizette and I would make it.

"Hurry!" Janey shouted as she heaved the heavy hatch open.

We heard a thump against the window and saw Cora, her skin mottled, discolored, and dissolving before our eyes. Seconds later, her entire body erupted into clouds of gaseous dust. Lizette and I looked at each other with fear in our eyes as we realized our fate.

Janey was down the hatch, yelling at us to get a move on it. Lizette looked at the phone in my hand and reached for hers to do the same thing I did. We'd go with Janey, but she would likely be the only one to leave if our rapidly color-changing skin was any indication. I stepped down onto the ladder that led down and started lowering my body into the darkness below. I moved slowly as I couldn't see anything. Once Lizette joined and pulled the hatch closed with her, sealing us away from the inside air, our eyesight plunged into blackness.

When my feet hit the ground, I activated the flashlight on my phone and held it up so Lizette had some light to see where to place her feet. Then, we silently followed Janey through the tunnel. I could feel the contagion spread across my body and was grateful that the dark tunnel hid it from view. The pain got worse and it wasn't long before my breathing matched Lizette's labored gasps.

A few minutes into our journey, we heard the facility's alarm blare out a warning designed to keep people away. It was an alarm that had never been activated before and signaled that the facility wasn't safe for humans to enter. Maybe it would be helpful to humankind if Lizette and I stayed in the confines of the tunnel. I didn't want to be ground zero for the rest of the world.

"Janey," I called out weakly. "You need to go. Get out and alert authorities that they need to evacuate the area within a ten-mile radius. Keep your suit on until you clear the safety area."

Janey stopped and turned around to look at me. I shined my phone flashlight on my face and her step faltered. I shook my head at her and waved her off. She needed to distance herself. There wasn't anything anyone could do for us now. Lizette and I braced ourselves against the side of the tunnel and watched Janey as she left with a whispered goodbye.

"Maybe if we stay back here, whatever this is won't get out into the air," Lizette wheezed as she sunk to the ground.

"That was my thought, too," I said as I followed her movement.

"Can you believe someone's vanity is why we are all dying?" Lizzete spat out in an angry whisper. "It's bullshit."

I agreed but didn't have the lung capacity to voice it. Instead, I reached for Lizette's hand and clutched it in mine. Fear had me not wanting to die alone. I didn't know what was happening to my insides; I only knew pain.

We bring you breaking news this afternoon about a dangerous virus unleashed at the medical research facility in the small town of Fredricksburg. The sirens signaling the town's danger was something people heard for miles, and authorities put an evacuation order into immediate effect. It was hours before a specialized unit deployed to the site. When our reporter reached the safety zone perimeter, authorities confirmed that no survivors remained within the facility.

The building's controls contained the contagion within the sealed building and we received word from a grieving spouse that the cause of this deadly disaster was due to an employee taking liberties with confidential research for their own gain. We have not been able to find the responsible party to get confirmation on this accusation, which could be that they were a victim inside the facility.

All that remains of the twenty-three on-site employees are empty clothes and moldy spores. Investigators confirmed the air was unbreathable and that they recovered contaminated remnants of eggshells throughout the facility, which are en route to a laboratory for forensic testing. It's a horrific and baffling scene in Fredricksburg. Our hearts go out to the families of those who perished today.

In other news, sightings across neighboring towns of a human-sized chicken wearing clothes spread across the internet in a viral wave as people posted videos on social media."

MAY

the Changeling

Bree Indigo

Once upon a time, in a kingdom far away, a young king and queen—neither wicked nor benign—wished for an heir. Each full moon, the king planted his seed in the fertile soil of the queen's garden, but each new moon the land remained barren.

The queen locked herself in the castle's tallest turret and sat by the window, watching as the leaves of the elm shading the castle that grew along the curtain wall turned first ochre, then sienna, finally making their descent—an inky, decaying shadow against the thin blanket of snow.

When winter came for the second time and still no seed had sprouted, the monarchs called upon the royal arborist, demanding with desperation an answer to their ailment. The arborist procured a tonic, an incantation, and instructions to return under the shadow of the next black moon.

The moon came, their majesties returned, and the arborist promised the pair: *This seed will bear you fruit.* Satisfied, the king left to fight a war in a kingdom across the sea, leaving the queen to prepare for the arrival of their heir.

The sprout broke through the soil in late spring—a small bud, barely formed—and by summer, a brilliant indigo flower had bloomed. Once more, the queen called upon the arborist who told her: *The fruit will be ripe by the first fall of snow.* A messenger was sent bringing good tidings to the king; his wife would soon bear a son.

Under a starless winter sky, the queen stood at her turret window staring into oblivion, waiting for the king's return, but the night was silent, and the sigh that escaped her lips formed a small cloud that quickly dissipated, leaving the queen to stare out into the vast, dark void once more. Suddenly she saw it—a single, perfect snowflake, making a slow, gentle descent into the queen's outstretched palm. *The prince is coming,* she whispered to the night.

With a roar, the queen brought her child into the world and after the royal arborist gently wiped away blood and earth, he presented the swaddled infant to the new mother. *The* princess, *your majesty.*

The king returned in the spring and the young rulers were overjoyed to have the heir they had wished for after so very long... But as the child grew, they realized she was not quite what they had expected.

She screamed for her mother, only to leave a ring of bite marks around the queen's neck, and snuck into the royal kennels in the deepest part of the night to touch the cats' eyes, which glittered like jewels in the darkness.

She was a wild thing, crushing berries and rosebuds in her fist, shouting at the sky with absolute abandon, running through puddles and rolling in the dirt, red clay streaked across her face and coating her dark, tangled hair until she appeared more golem than child.

The monarchs brought her to court dressed in ivory and gold, her hair in perfect spiral curls, and presented her to the other nobility. *This is our daughter, Briar Rose.* But when she met the other children, the girls were afraid to stain their dresses with paint or mud, preferring tea parties and dolls, while the boys snickered and shoved her, proclaiming: *We don't play with girls.* She knew she would never, ever be one of them.

When Briar began to bloom two winters earlier than her mother predicted, the arborist was summoned and arrived in haste under the light of a pale full moon ringed with blood. He assured the queen: *This happens, sometimes.* Though, as Briar grew older and more winters passed, she would go many months between blooming, unlike the other young ladies of the royal court who bloomed each moon like clockwork.

If the king had been disappointed in his lack of a son, he never showed it, though Briar Rose always wished he would invite her for the annual Wild Hunt, like all the sons riding alongside their fathers. The queen was loving though mercurial, quick to criticize, often indifferent but somehow always disappointed.

Briar found her sanctuary far from the judgmental stares of the monarchs and court, deep in the west wing and nestled in an alcove, in the furthest reaches of the royal library, surrounded by her favorite books; here she was alone but never lonely, head and heart filled with stories who became her most trusted companions.

One day, while buried in *The Cryptid Compendium,* she encountered a chapter she'd never read, though the tattered tome was a favorite. The story told of the changeling—a faerie child left in place of a stolen baby, raised by human parents who were often none the wiser. Though, sometimes, when a child was strange—unusual and curious, sickly but ravenous, wise beyond their years, delighted in destruction—sometimes, the changeling would be found out, tested and revealed by fire, eggshells, or iron.

Briar stared at her hand for a long moment, then caught her own gaze reflected in the dark window: her eyes haunted, skin pale and ghostly, tangled dark curls a wild silhouette.

She gathered the tome against her chest, easily navigating the dimly lit maze of bookshelves and towering stacks, quickly retracing her steps to her private quarters. She rummaged through drawers, finding delicate hair pins and the heavy sewing scissors that once belonged to her grandmother.

Holding a hair pin between two fingers, she regarded it carefully, but the metal was soft, bending under pressure and she frowned; the elegant pin was silver. The scissors were sturdy and seemed ancient, like they had always been and always would be, but Briar's frown remained, certain the scissors couldn't be silver or copper or gold, but unclear how to discern between steel and iron. She pressed the cold metal against the warm, pale skin of her wrist and forearm; the dull blade elicited goosebumps, but nothing else.

Moonlight guided her path as Briar snuck out, past the kennels with their jewel-eyed cats, through the rose garden and the berry orchard, past the royal arboretum to the stables where most of the chickens nested high in the rafters above the other animals. She pulled an egg out from under a broody hen who pecked Briar half-heartedly, then clucked and resettled on her clutch of eggs while Briar lit a candle, quickly checking to make sure the egg wasn't growing, and cracked the shell carefully into two halves, letting the yolk run out onto the earth as she retraced her steps back to the rose garden.

Her reflection in the birdbath was clear, like fine glass, and the night was still, as if every living thing was watching and holding its breath with her, the tension thick as she dipped the shells and her trembling hands into the water. She closed her eyes, lifting the eggshells above her head, letting the water run down her face and hair in cold rivulets, then Briar exhaled, ready to see her true self revealed... But when she forced her eyes open, the face reflected hadn't changed and Briar crushed the eggshells in her fists, throwing them into the grass, a frustrated sound escaping her throat.

Laying in bed, Briar watched the moon cross the cobalt sky through her window before it sank into the obsidian tree line. As the sun finally began to rise, a spark ignited—small at first, barely a firefly, but quickly catching fire.

Spring broke through suddenly that year, tulip and daffodil buds bursting through melting snow and the castle transformed. Russet buds gave way to new leaves and chains of tiny blossoms decorating the giant oak tree while lush, exotic grass and vibrant blooms filled the courtyards.

Sitting by the gnarled old elm, Briar perched atop the curtain wall, watching the castle bustle about as she had each Midsummer's Day since she was small, taking in the brilliant colored ribbons woven around the Maypole, the air perfumed by the multitudes of ochre flowers adorning the castle halls and courtyards and stacks of firewood awaiting tonight's festivities.

With a small, resigned sigh, Briar lowered herself down the stone wall and out of bounds, into the thick, thorny brush below.

The sun was making its slow descent, casting a golden glow through the moss that drenched the birch and maple trees surrounding Briar and she was mesmerized by the pure, raw beauty all around her. Almost enchanted by the path beneath her leather boots, she soon realized she was losing the light and wouldn't escape the forest before nightfall.

Fear rose in her throat and rang in her ears as Briar tried to find her way through shadow and silhouette, branches reaching toward her like strangers, grabbing at her skirts and cloak until finally Briar screamed, a wordless fury ripping up through her chest and out her throat.

Hunched over, her breath ragged, the young woman began to laugh—a thin giggle at first, spilling and breaking, until she was cackling, her head thrown back in wild abandon.

What am I so afraid of? I don't fear death or an ending. Let the wolves take me and tear the marrow from my bones.

Darkness broke, a thin haze of clouds parting to reveal the goddess Selene in her full splendor as Briar crested the hill, leaving the shadows and forest behind her.

At the edge of the village, a small bonfire blazed and Briar edged closer, the flames writhing and snapping. She found she could not look away, even as the heat licked her face. Would it burn her hollow? Strip flesh from bone and reveal what she truly was? Her breath shallow and eyes wild, Briar leaned forward, waiting for the fire to choose.

Flames leapt, clawing skyward as a face split the fire, mouth gaping in a silent scream then vanishing into smoke and shadow and Briar shrieked, stumbling backward, crashing hard into–

A woman, eyes blue like the chicory blooms and

forget-me-nots growing in the royal arboretum, her auburn hair alight with the glow of the bonfire.

Briar scrambled, afraid she was caught, but the woman only bared her teeth in a grin. *Join me,* the other woman bade, not mocking nor cruel, but sure and unshaken, offering a delicate hand to Briar. *Come through the fire,* the stranger added and Briar's own voice echoed in her mind, cutting through any hesitation: *What am I so afraid of?*

She took the woman's hand and leapt.

What is Inside Me?

Nathan Sykes

I could hear my grandma's voice, but her voice was a distant, muffled sound, as if we were separated by walls of pillows. I watched the neighbors from my perch on her soft floral-patterned couch, the slits of the window's blinds my only glimpse of the foreign world I inhabited... a little place called Littleton, Colorado. It was June, and the sky was a radiant blanket of deep blue. Like the ocean, it felt like I could fall in and sink forever if I stared toward the cloudless abyss for too long. Everything moved slowly there, unlike every other aspect of my life. I watched families pack camping gear into the cars, fathers mowing their lawns or washing their cars while mothers read a book or knitted on the porch, and I watched their kids run wildly up and down the street. The kids were always outside... the street was littered with little gangs of children playing all day, every day. I wondered what that felt like... they all seemed so happy in ways I'd never seen before.

"Hello!" My grandma's slightly raised voice finally brought me from my trance, the word rolling off her tongue as crisp as the chilly morning air in the fall. "Jennifer, sweetie... anyone home?"

It took some effort, but I managed to pull my attention from the window to look at my exasperated grandmother. "Sorry Grammy," I said, truly feeling terrible once I realized I'd been completely ignoring her the whole time. She tilted her head and gave me that doubtful look, like she suspected I was just reading from a script or something.

"I'm sure your parents didn't send you here for the summer just so you can sink into that cushion feeling sorry for yourself while you live vicariously through the neighbors..."

"Vi-curious?" I was twelve, and Grammy thought my youthful ignorance was hilarious. I wasn't used to it at all. I only met my grandparents a handful of times before, but they were family, and I loved them very much. I heard their voices over the phone all the time, and they sent me gifts and cards full of money for every holiday. I was happy to be there, and I really did feel bad.

"Vicarious." She corrected when she finished chuckling. "Means to experience something through someone else... which is not the way to spend your summer vacation!" she added sternly. "You should go out there and make some friends... enjoy the weather! Go get into trouble! Kiss a boy!"

"Eww! Gross!" I squealed at the thought, and she grinned through another hearty laugh. "Grammy... I don't know how to make friends. I stopped trying since—"

"Oh please!" she retorted. "You kids are easy! Just go be nice and give someone a compliment, or ask if you can play! Your dad can't help that his job moves him around so much! He's a very important Navy man," she said as she smiled and ruffled my hair, and I couldn't help but giggle. I loved her so much... it was like she always knew what to do or say, even if it wasn't what I wanted to hear at the time, and she did it all out of love. I always knew that. "...but that doesn't mean," she rolled up her sleeves and grabbed me by my shoulders, "that you should miss out on being a kid!"

"But—" I started to protest, but she would hear none of it.

She led me to the front door and shoved me across the threshold. "Go have some fun sweetie!" I barely heard her shut the door behind me as I stepped out onto the soft grass of her front yard, the smell of her flowerbed and a neighbor's barbecue greeting my nostrils. All I heard was the birds chirping, the spray of hose water or sprinklers, some music coming from someone's garage, and kids playing... their screams of summer joy, the sound of children's freedom I'd never known until then.

A group of kids around my age were riding their bikes past my grandparent's house. "Wait up guys!" A little girl called after them. She must've been around eight or nine. She was pedaling that bike fiercely trying to keep up with the older kids, but she was never going to catch up. She stopped in the street out front, looked over at me and smiled. I waved and she returned the gesture. "Are you new here?" she asked me.

I told her I was just there for the summer, and she commented on how the older kids that left her behind were jerks. "Do you have an older brother or sister?" she asked me. I told her I was the only child. She rolled her eyes and told me I was lucky. I didn't feel very lucky.

"Are you kidding?" I retorted. "What I'd give to have a brother or sister. I think you're the lucky one!"

"Yeah, my brother's pretty great!" She was beaming up at me. "I'm Riley by the way." Her hair was done up in pigtails, and over her typical little kid clothes she wore what

I could only assume was one of her older brother's jackets because the sleeves were rolled up nearly half way, and the jacket hung past her butt. I thought it was cute though.

"I'm Jennifer—" Just as I was introducing myself to Riley, the other kids showed back up. I wanted to shrink away and simply vanish in that moment. They were all staring at me like I had a tentacle growing out of my forehead. It had been so long since I bothered talking to anyone that I didn't know what to say, and we all just stared at each other for what felt like way too long. Finally, the only other girl of the group other than Riley, came to my rescue. She looked around at the boys and shook her head.

"Y'all are so dumb." She laughed. "As if I'm not a girl..." She had glasses on and was wearing overalls that were cutoff above the knees, a tank top underneath, and her hair was up in a ponytail... what hadn't come out anyway, which wasn't much.

"You're such a total nerd..." the freckled redhead wearing a shirt that read 'have I ever faked a sarcasm?' blurted out. "That's doesn't count!" Everyone laughed, even the girl, who shrugged, and the tension seemed to melt away after that.

"We're headed to the lake," the tallest of the group said. He was wearing a basketball jersey and sneakers... the kind you'd wear to the gym. "Wanna tag along?" The other boys all looked at him for a moment before looking back at me.

"Sure!" I said enthusiastically, happy that I might've already made some friends. "But I don't have a bike."

"Hop on Jace's pegs. We'll go grab you one." A boy with scruffy hair that poked out from a baseball cap said. Only one of them had pegs on their bike. He was wearing a cheap pleather jacket and ripped jeans.

The boy with the baseball cap was Alex. If the group had a leader it was him. He was always coming up with the plans, and knew exactly how to best use everyone's unique set of skills, directing us throughout the summer like he was playing a game of chess. The girl with the glasses was Zoe. The redhead, Mitch, wasn't joking when he'd called her a nerd. She was always in the middle of conducting some sort of science experiment whenever we swung by her house, and sketching things in a notepad she carried everywhere. Mitch was always making everyone laugh. Most of the time he was a proper comedian, but sometimes his jokes were very poorly timed. We'd all laugh about that later on though. The one with the basketball jersey was Kyler. His parents put him in all the sports, and he was really good at them. He kind of resented them at the same time, but I don't think he knew it back then. Then there was Jace, the outcast and rebel of the group. Before I showed up, he was the newest of the group. He was from the outskirts of town and wanted nothing to do with the others, but they eventually won him over. He always acted like he didn't care about anything, but deep down he was a big softy. Riley was Alex's little sister. He couldn't go anywhere without her, but she brought a lot of energy to the group. Her small stature came in handy a lot as well.

We ended up at a small junk yard. We snuck in through a hole in the fence and Alex knew exactly where to go. He brought us to a beat-up bicycle, which for the most part, wasn't in terrible condition other than needing some replacement parts. He gave everyone a part to find and the group scattered. Jace got a hold of some tools, and pretty soon he was getting to work. It wasn't long before I had my very own bike to ride, and we were off to the lake, where Mitch pulled a bunch of snacks out of his backpack and passed them around. They adopted me into the group without a second thought about it, and I hung out with them every day throughout the remainder of the summer. We went on so many adventures that summer, and every summer after.

One time we snuck into an old abandoned mine to explore, and somehow the entrance collapsed behind us. We were stuck in there for hours. It was a maze, but Alex used his compass to keep us moving in the right direction, and kept everyone calm and collected. He was always the bravest of the group, but more often than not, his bravery was what got us in bizarre situations to begin with. He was always there to get us out of them though. Turned out that some bullies caused the entrance to collapse behind us. We figured that out on a different occasion when we were all hanging out at a local swimming hole and they showed up talking crap. They were calling me names, and then Zoe and Riley as well, and started throwing rocks down the bank toward us as we treaded water. After some of us nearly got hit by some big ones a few times, Jace hit one of them square in the chest with a rock of his own using a slingshot he always had sticking out of his pants. He surprised us all since he typically avoided confrontations, and we all cheered for him when he hit them two or three other times while warning them to back off, and the bullies took off crying.

Over the years we all had our time to shine. As a group, we followed Zoe's directions and helped her build a rocket for a summer science festival, where she took home the grand prize. Another summer we helped her make a go-kart, which the group voted Alex would co-pilot with her in that summer's races. They ended up winning second place, but got first place on a technicality when the judges discovered the other winners had cheated in the construction of their go-kart. Anytime Kyler had a game, we all went to support him, and his teams won games more often than not. One summer he also climbed a ravine and saved a little kid's life who had fallen trying to rescue a stray cat that had wandered into a quarry. He was awarded yet another trophy to add to his collection for that. Mitch was always there to lighten the mood anytime we got ourselves in a scary situation. It's amazing what a little laughter can do for morale. As we got older, he started going to open mic nights in town, and I got to watch one of my best friends make half the town laugh their pants off. The bullies stopped bothering us when Mitch got really good at quick witted comebacks. I was the musician of the group. Anytime we got to lay under the stars or sit around a campfire, I would sing, when Zoe wasn't teaching us all about the constellations that is.

Everything changed the summer I was sixteen. I'd met all their families many times before, but only Jace's on a few occasions. His older brother Casey was always really nice, and really cool. He had long wavy hair and always wore band tees and plaid shirts with the sleeves torn off. He reminded me of Jace in a lot of ways. He played the guitar though, and asked me every time I saw him to sing while he played, but I was always too nervous. We didn't know at the time, but anytime our group got into trouble, Casey took the blame and received the brunt of Jace's punishments. Still, he never took it out on any of us. He'd have some sarcastic comments to make every now and then regarding our escapades, but he was always looking out for Jace and, by extension, the rest of the group. One night after we'd all hung out at Jace's, his dad offered to drive everyone home. I was the last to be dropped off.

"So," he started, "you and Jace ever...?"

The question caught me off guard. I was so uncomfortable, but what was I supposed to do? "No." I answered him.

He made a *humm* sound and nodded. "I don't see why not." He retorted. "Y'all have aged so fast." He looked over at me, and I watched his eyes go up and down slowly as he scanned over my entire body. My entire nervous system screamed at me, and I felt weak like I was going to be sick. I thought my heart had sank into my stomach. He licked his lips as his eyes lingered on my chest. "You've grown into a very fine-looking girl, Jenny."

I wanted to scream. I wanted to unbuckle my seatbelt and jump out of the car as he drove down the street, but I couldn't move. I could hardly breathe. I held back my tears, not wanting to appear weak or afraid... I didn't want to upset him, so I thanked him. Speaking the words made my throat close up. He smiled at me. "You should come over more often," he told me. "I think you'd brighten the place up, what'ya say, Jenny?"

The car came to a stop in front of my grandparent's house and he slid his arm across the back of the passenger seat, and every hair on my body stood on end when he placed it upon my back. "Yeah..." I tried not to stutter or let my voice crack with fear. "...maybe. That might be fine... I'd have to ask—"

"Oh no need, sweetie," he said with a smooth, sultry tone. "I've already spoken with your grandparents, and they agree that it sounds like a fine idea." I tried to hide the utter terror from my face as I reached for the door handle. I opened the door and began scooting off the seat, away from his reach, and onto my feet outside the car. His eyes never left mine. "Be seein' ya around, Jenny," he said as he waved at me, smiling that sickening smile of his. I was frozen... couldn't move, and I just stood there looking at him, screaming at myself in my head to *move! Run inside!* He leaned over, grabbed the handle, and shut the passenger door before driving away. I cried myself to sleep that night, terrified of ever leaving that house again... and I didn't leave that house, not for days and days.

I told my grandparents I wasn't feeling well, but I knew it wouldn't last. I didn't know what to do. Then one night I heard pebbles hitting my window. My friends were out there. They were worried about me. I felt my life crumbling around me and I wanted the comfort of my friends more than anything in that moment, but I was scared. We all made eye contact and I closed the curtains. That was it, I thought... the happiest part of my life had come to an end, and I spent the next couple days deciding I was going to go home early, but then...

"Knock-knock," my grandma said as she opened my bedroom door. "There's a boy at the front door for you, honey." Boy? I wondered which one it could be, but I would've never guessed correctly. It was Casey. Seeing his face caught me so off guard, and I realized something... I was relieved to see him and not any of the others. I was glad it was him. I didn't really understand why, but his presence made me feel a lot better. Before I could stop myself, I had thrown my arms around him, and nearly burst into tears. I looked back at my grandma as if to ask for permission to leave the house. She smiled and nodded.

We walked aimlessly and talked for a while. I would've gone home and never gone back if it wasn't for Casey. He made me feel seen and heard... he made me feel safe. I told him what happened and he was livid. I made him promise he wouldn't do anything stupid, and he protected me the rest of that summer. We grew closer and spent more time together that summer and the next... we even spoke more throughout the year between my trips to Littleton than the rest of the group and I did. We even kind of dated for a time, but long distance was never going to work. I'd often dreamed of moving there after I turned eighteen, but the truth is... my summers in Littleton helped with my confidence. My friends made me feel like it was okay to make other friends without the fear of losing them, and I just so happened to spend the entirety of my high school experience at the same school. My last trip was after graduation. I went to college that fall and just got busy with life. We all did. We still keep in touch from time to time though.

I went back to visit after five years. It had been a while since any of us had spoken, but we were all really enthusiastic about catching up, and I was a little nervous to see Casey. Even though he had never officially been part of the group, I knew nobody would object to him being part of the reunion. He'd not just been my protector after all, but he'd looked out for all of us for years. We were all catching up and drinking around a bonfire, like the good old days minus the alcohol. Nobody batted an eye about Riley drinking either, even though she was only twenty. Who cared? It wasn't that, but something... something didn't feel right to me. I couldn't have explained it had I tried, but it was as if my mind had fractured all of a sudden, like I was either waking up from a very vivid and wild dream, or tripping on something. I don't do drugs, and I was definitely awake so it wasn't either of those. I opened all my own drinks so nobody spiked the alcohol. I was really confused and started looking around frantically.

"Everything okay, Jennifer?" Jace asked. The others looked at me concerned then.

"Yeah..." I stammered, trying to pinpoint what exactly felt wrong. I met the eyes of all my friends: Alex, Riley, Mitch, Zoe, Jace, Kyler... and... "Where's..." I said as I looked each of my friends in the face, unable to shake the feeling something was off... "Where's your brother?" I finally finished.

"My brother?" Jace asked, a puzzled expression across his face.

"Casey?" I scoffed. "Yeah! Your brother, Casey!" Everyone looked at me as if I'd lost my mind.

"Casey isn't my brother... he's my neighbor," Jace answered. "Are you okay, Jenn?"

I could feel my face get red hot. "That isn't funny!" I barked at him.

"Yeah, Jace..." Kyler spoke up. I looked at him, relieved it wasn't just me. "Casey isn't your neighbor... he lives in my neighborhood..."

What the fuck was going on...

"I thought Casey was your cousin, Alex?" Zoe spoke up.

"What?" Alex asked in surprise.

"He isn't..." Riley said.

"Guys... what the fuck!?" I screamed. "I came here every summer for years! I've always known him to be Jace's older brother! This isn't fucking funny!" I was furious! I was confused and hurt. I didn't know what kind of game they were playing with me, but I'd had enough. "Is this some kind of sick joke you're all pulling on me? Why? Because I had a thing for him and none of you?"

"Real nice, Jenn..." Jace retorted as he and the

other boys stared incredulously at me.

"Guys!" Zoe snapped. "Enough! Obviously—"

I pulled out my phone to call Casey and... "...the hell?" I couldn't find his number anywhere. Our text conversation wasn't there either. It was like he was erased from my phone altogether. "Check your phones! I can't find him in mine... but I know I've talked to him... I know I had his number saved."

Everyone checked their phones and he was missing from all of theirs as well. We spent the entire evening trying to get to the bottom of who Casey really was. None of us remembered him the same way. He wasn't related to any of them, and yet my memories were so clear. We tried looking for old pictures of us, but Casey wasn't really ever there. He covered for us all the time, and got in trouble a lot because of it, but he never really joined us on our little misadventures. Mitch thought he found one of him, but it was the back of someone's head, and it definitely wasn't Casey. The person he pointed out had short blonde hair, but Casey... *my* Casey has long wavy brown hair.

This was all wrong.

We all remembered him looking different. We remembered how he dressed differently. The more we talked about Casey the more we forgot about him. I couldn't remember what color eyes he has... how was that possible? As hard as I tried, I couldn't recall the sound of his voice, and I knew his voice better than any of them! Except for Jace, perhaps. The more we investigated Casey, the more of a stranger he became, even though we all remember there being a Casey around... not all the time or even consistently, but a big presence Zoe nonetheless. I mean, he was the reason I never went home that summer! He was the reason we were all still friends! So how was it... it was like he never existed?

How did we all remember someone named Casey?

As the night continued and we were all hyper fixated on the mystery surrounding Casey, our memories of him got stranger and stranger, as if he was somehow implanting bizarre experiences into our minds to throw us all off his trail like some sort of phantom parasite. Alex had a memory of Casey helping him put Christmas lights up on his house in one of the hottest summers of the past decade. Mitch remembered a time Casey dumped an enormous pile of forks on the floor during one of his stand-ups. Zoe remembered a time he stood outside her house and did jumping jacks all night. It was as if we'd always remembered these things, yet were only then able to recall them. Then a memory came back to me, and my blood ran cold... the memory was so vivid. Casey had confronted his father, or Jace's father over what had happened. He threatened Casey... his own son in my mind... for weeks the man made Casey's life a living hell, and then... I remembered the night Casey confided in me. He had nobody else to turn to; nobody he trusted more than me. It was so real... my heart leaped into my throat as the memory played out in my head, then sank into my gut and stopped beating as I realized I'd kept it secret all these years... that Casey murdered his and Jace's father to protect us both. I keeled over puking and dry heaving. My whole body was trembling. This couldn't be real... I had to be dreaming! This had to be a nightmare, and I just needed to wake up.

Alex thought it was best that the seven of us went back to stay with his and Riley's parents for the night. She was still living with them for one, but he argued we needed a lighter atmosphere, that their parents would be over the moon to see me. He also said I needed food and rest, and the group would be able to take better care of me there. I wanted to ask Jace about his dad so bad, but I think part of me didn't want the confirmation, even though deep down I knew it to be true. Their parents were very happy to see me, and eventually the night seemed to take a lighter tone, but I could tell we were all still very spooked about the whole thing under the mask... we just chose to pretend like everything was perfectly fine. I fell asleep with a heavy heart, unsure what to do about the awful new memory.

We woke to the smell of bacon, sausage and french toast the next morning. My stomach rumbled angrily at me, as if I'd neglected it for days. The seven of us groggily made our way to the dining room where a fresh pot of coffee waited for us... thank god!

As we sipped and woke up, Alex and Riley's mom looked around at us smiling. "Awww..." She cooed with a hint of disappointment. "Did Casey take off already?" A bunch of us spat our coffee out in disbelief and just stared at her. She thought it was funny while maintaining her disappointment, and then squinted at me with a devious smirk on her face. "You two love birds are so adorable you know! Watching the two of you last night reminded me..."

Her voice faded from my world as I struggled to register her words. Casey had been with us all night... I remembered now... but he wasn't. We all stared wide-eyed at one another. None of us said anything as Alex and Riley's mom dished out our food... to eight plates... "Are you... are you joining us?" I asked their mom, feigning a smile. It wasn't like her to eat with us. She always waited until everyone else had finished eating.

"Oh no, dear," she said, smiling. "I can wait. You lot have your fill first." Once there was food on every plate, she left us to it.

"Do you guys remember him being with us last

night?" I asked aloud once she'd left the room. They did, but again, their memories of Casey were jumbled. "How many plates do you guys count?"

"Eight," Zoe replied. They all counted eight.

I began counting my friends and I. There should be seven of us in total, but despite not seeing Casey there, I kept counting eight. "How many of us are you guys counting?" My voice shook as I asked.

"Eight..." Again, they all counted eight. It was as if he was still with us right then and there. As if he'd been with us the whole time. Then I remembered our kiss... the affection we shared... the intimacy the night before...

I realize how crazy this sounds, and I don't know how to explain it, but my friends and I grew up with someone who never existed... yet he haunts us with his continued presence. He's never there in the moment, but shows up in the memories afterward. I don't know what's fact or fiction anymore. I'm losing my mind... I'm paranoid as shit, and there's nothing I can do... nowhere I can go to get away from Casey. The thought of him makes me sick, but also fills me with warmth and butterflies simultaneously. The others have just accepted that Casey is a thing that exists yet doesn't exist, and they don't bring him up anymore, but he doesn't get personal with them. How am I supposed to ignore him when he is infatuated with me?

...when I am carrying his child?

JULY

Always Recycle

Lauren Patzer

As the printer pushed out the latest receipt, Julia Benson smiled at her spreadsheet on the monitor. *One more project and we should eliminate plastic entirely from all the packaging with no extra cost,* she mused.

She looked out her office window at the dusty air rising up in the distance over the scattered corporate office complexes filling the valley and sighed. It was July, when the heat would make the plastic floating in the seas and rivers the most toxic. As the chemicals leeched out into the surrounding water, it was just another reminder that everything including humanity had an expiration date. They could only delay the inevitable so far, but at least they were slowing the progression.

As Julia reached for the page sitting in the output bin, a man she didn't recognize with dark, slick and meticulously styled hair walked in. He grabbed the sheet from under her fingers and scoffed at it. Julia frowned as she took the man in. His three-piece suit reeked of corporate executive suite stench all the way down to his dyed and polished alligator skin shoes.

"You Benson?" he asked as he pointed a corner of the printed receipt at her.

"Doctor Benson. And you are?" she replied coolly as she pointed at the door. He glanced at the name on the door and chuckled. It read 'Doctor Julia Benson, Director Materials Research."

"Yeah, another uppity ho," he murmured.

"Excuse me?" Julia asked as she stood up.

He looked back at her and smiled. "The name is Franklin Peele, new CEO."

"What happened to Mister Turing?" she asked.

"The board is taking a new, more profitable direction. Don't worry, I've done this before. Come in, cut the chaff, improve the profits."

"Well then, you'll be pleased to know we just attained zero plastics in the packing for the generators here. That's at no extra cost and immeasurable benefit to the environment."

"Yeah, yeah. I've seen the numbers. I've already rerouted that project to a new plastics startup, resulting in one percent cost reduction over the last packaging design."

"With a considerable black eye to the company's reputation, Mister Peele. Korling Mechanical has spent a large sum advertising the renewable efforts of the company to great acclaim from the industry and the stockholders," Julia replied as she folded her arms in front of her.

Peele grinned and Julia couldn't help but feel disgusted by it. He turned and shut the door, giving the two of them an immediately uncomfortable level of privacy. When he turned to face her again, his artificially pleasant demeanor disappeared.

"I repeat—I'm here to cut the chaff. That means all the useless space taken by women in this company. You're the last one who hasn't been let go. That ends now. Pack your things and go." He tossed an envelope on the desk addressed to her.

"Doesn't HR normally handle this task?" Julia responded as she picked up the envelope.

"As you're a woman of some reputation, I wanted to handle this one personally. The world doesn't need some shit for brains bitch poking her nose in the running of businesses. That's the realm of men. You really want to be useful? Find a man, lay on your back for him, do his bidding and keep your bitch mouth shut. That's what women are good for."

"I'm inclined to disagree, Mister Peele," she said coolly as she opened a drawer and retrieved her car keys.

"I don't care what you agree with, psycho bitch. Just get the fuck out." Franklin replied nonchalantly, as if he was ordering a cup of coffee.

"Psycho?" Julia replied with a chuckle. "Why, no one has called me that in years. Thank you."

"Thank you?" Franklin repeated with a frown as she walked by him.

She unclipped her corporate badge and handed it to him as she opened the door. "You've inspired me to revisit an old recycling program I haven't used in a while. Time to fire it back up."

Julia turned her back on Franklin and strolled away.

"Well, good riddance, psycho," he murmured as he put her badge in his pocket and went on to the next office. "God, I love this fucking job."

A week later, Franklin smiled as he reviewed his bank account. True to their word, Korling Mechanical's board gave him a generous bonus for his streamlining of the company. Firing all the higher paid, experienced employees gutted the brain trust of the company, but resulted in lower projected costs. In a few years, the company would be essentially worthless as there was no one left to innovate and access new markets or acquire new customers, but that wasn't why they hired Franklin. He existed solely to gut the company, as he'd done to many other companies. Only the chairman of the board knew Franklin's true purpose—to make the company ripe for a hostile takeover, exposing their valuable patents for a song. The newer, weaker company would be ready for poaching within a few months. The chairman would profit handsomely through a privately held, third party corporation.

Of course, Franklin would be out of the company by then, having pocketed his generous bonuses and a few hefty paychecks before leaving the disaster he'd created behind to start the process all over again at another rich target.

Six months passed. Franklin walked into his latest board meeting with Gypsy Chemicals and gave the entire board their walking papers. In just a few months, he decimated three companies altogether. There were shouts and curses, but the stockholders had made their desires clear. Increase profits at any cost. His unspoken goal was making it ripe to be plundered, this time by himself instead of some chairman of the board mole. The company-ending losses were something the stockholders never signed up for but would be powerless to stop.

As newly hired security escorted the former board members from the property, Franklin walked to the window and glanced down at his reserved, CEO parking spot, expecting to land eyes on his yellow Lamborghini. His jaw dropped open when he saw it wasn't there. He rushed to his office and stood in front of his assistant's desk.

"Get me the head of security!" Franklin screamed at him. The younger man cocked his head.

"Do you mean the head of the five-man goon squad you hired this morning?" he asked as he scratched his head, temporarily dislodged a few slick hairs. When he put his hand back down, the hair immediately fell back into place.

"No, I mean..." Franklin's anger turned into a groan.

The assistant turned his notebook around and showed Franklin the written list. "The same playbook every time, Mister Peele. The only ones left in the building are me, you and the goon squad."

"We ended the security camera contract last week," Franklin said and sighed. "Well, contact the boys in blue and tell them there's been a robbery."

"What's left to steal?"

"My car is missing, Danny."

"The Lambo? Maybe somebody moved it as a prank. You know, like the last company moved your entire office into the men's room." Franklin rolled his eyes.

"Can't hurt to take a quick look around, right?" Danny asked.

Franklin nodded and Danny joined him as they walked to the elevator.

"I gotta hand it to you, boss," Danny said. "You're amazing."

"I know."

"Look, I gotta know how you do it."

"Be amazing?" Franklin scoffed.

"Sure, that's part of it. No, I mean, how do you keep Mary from finding out about Linda and Gina? Heck, how do you keep them all from finding out about each other?"

"Ah, Danny. You assume I care if any of them find

out about one another."

Danny's eyes got wide.

"Women are just a tool. A hole, really, for my tool," he said with a chuckle. "I just use them for my sexual gratification. When I'm tired of them, I boot them out the door. You have them scheduled at six, eight, and ten tonight, right?"

"Yeah, yeah, of course. But what if you want to marry one of them?" Danny asked.

"That will never happen. I keep my girls pure. They've signed agreements to have procedures done if any of them should become pregnant. When you have the money, you have the power in the relationship. Remember that."

"Right," Danny replied as he nodded.

"These women came from nothing and that's what they'll return to."

"But, you pay them, don't you?"

"They each have an allowance; just enough to keep them solvent. I have people tracking their accounts. When they build up savings that might allow them to leave, I make sure something 'happens' to keep them on the edge of poverty. Flat tire, dog gets sick or maybe a little fire at one of their close relatives' houses. Just little things to have them shelling out whatever they can spare to cover the expense. Always maintain the power in the relationship, Danny. Never let those wastrels gain the upper hand."

"Wastrels?" Danny frowned.

"Come on, Danny, use that big brain of yours to keep up on ways to demean women. It's what makes life worth living." Franklin smiled as the door dinged. The elevator doors opened and the two men walked out through the foyer into the parking lot. They walked the short distance to the CEO parking spot. There was a piece of paper held down by a thick rectangle of clear plastic. Franklin reached down and picked them both up.

The plastic was about the size of a bar of soap and looked to be some kind of clear epoxy. Embedded in the plastic was one of his business cards from Gypsy Chemicals. The paper was on the company's letterhead with one simple sentence printed on it: Thank you for recycling.

"Is this some kind of game?" Danny asked.

"Someone's playing a game all right. It ends now. Call the cops," Franklin said.

"Well, they didn't take kindly to your last call about the missing office furniture," Danny replied.

"Never mind. I'll do it myself," Franklin replied. "You're fired."

"What? But I—"

"Did I stutter?!" Franklin shouted at Danny.

"Fine," Danny replied. He walked to his car across the empty parking lot.

Franklin dialed 911 on his phone. "Fucking idiot," Franklin muttered.

Danny climbed into his car and started it up. As he drove out of the parking lot, the emergency services dispatcher answered the phone.

"Nine one one, what's your emergency?" a woman asked.

"My car was stolen," Franklin replied.

"Is anyone injured?"

"No."

"Is there a fire or other danger to human life?" the woman asked in a perfectly neutral tone.

"No, but my Lamborghini Revuelto has been stolen," Franklin replied with the annoyance rising in his voice.

"Sir, you'll need to call the non-emergency hotline. The number is—"

"Listen, bitch!" Franklin screamed at the phone. "You get cops down here right now or I will cleave the hair from your scalp with a hatchet!"

There was a pause.

"My apologies, sir. What is your name and what is the address?"

Franklin calmed down and gave her his name and the address.

"The police will be there shortly." She replied and hung up.

It took about five minutes for Franklin to hear the sirens. It was another three minutes before the two squad cars screeched to a halt mere feet away from him. After drawing their weapons and ordering him onto the ground, Franklin was cuffed, read his rights and whisked away from the office building.

After Franklin was strip searched, booked and handed prison garb, he spent several hours in a holding cell with three other detainees who all kept their own clothing. His cell mates were all released before the fuming private equity genius got his obligatory phone call. He called his lawyer, John Alston. He waited on hold for several minutes.

"Franklin?" John asked.

"Yes! Why did it take so long—you know what, never mind. Just *get me out of here.*" Franklin swallowed hard, pushing down his anger.

"Why are you calling me? You fired my firm last week," John replied.

"What?"

"Our accounts receivable clerk, Brenda, called your

number to renew your retainer, which had run out. She got an answering service that informed us our services were no longer needed."

"Wait, what about the Kellings merger?"

"It didn't happen. We'd already gone over on billable hours and, since I couldn't reach you personally, I had to abandon the case. You used to be on top of your affairs, but it seems you've gotten lazy or forgetful recently. I recommend you see a doctor."

"Look, John—" Franklin stopped when he heard the dial tone. It took a few moments to process the slight by his long time lawyer. He slammed the phone receiver angrily on the table until it broke in half, moments before the guards grabbed his arms and hauled him back to the holding cell.

He spent the night there and walked into a courtroom the next morning for an arraignment with a public defender. He got a trial date and given a bond of ten thousand dollars. While his new lawyer argued this was his client's first offense, the judge noted he committed multiple offenses, including destruction of county property—the jail's phone. Franklin thanked the judge for his understanding and meekly walked from the courtroom, escorted by the bailiff to the accounts receivable clerk.

Franklin used his exclusive black credit card to post bail. He walked out of the courtroom in his day old clothing, reeking of sweat and old jail cell. He called a limousine service to pick him up and put a rush on it at considerable expense. His favorite whiskey and a basket full of sandwiches awaited him when he climbed into the back of the long, black vehicle.

The half hour trip home gave Franklin time to relax and recover his senses. He nearly felt like himself again when the limousine stopped in front of his estate and he climbed out. He shut the car door behind him and the rented vehicle pulled away, off to its next assignment. As he walked up the long driveway, his eyes caught something unusual sitting just outside his front door. A cube of crushed metal and yellow fiberglass sat there with little bits scattered around it on the red brick pavement.

A small rectangular sliver of metal stuck out from the mass; Franklin pulled it out. It was the license plate from his Lamborghini.

"Who would do this?" he whispered. His thoughts poured over the years of activity since he'd started raiding companies. He shook his head.

"Barrington. Simon Barrington. He nearly cried when I removed him from his father's company. This is personal. It's got to be him," Franklin said.

He threw the license plate on the ground and strode to his front door. He twisted the doorknob, but it wouldn't budge. Something felt off. He looked down at the door handle and noticed the flat blue ring around the shank. Below it hung a combination lock box.

"No..." Franklin whispered. He pulled his key out and tried it in the lock. It wouldn't fit. He stumbled over to the garage door and tried that doorknob, but found it locked as well. Punching in his combination to the digital locks just gave him a blinking red light. He ran around the considerably large house and found each door secured. He glanced through the rear French doors into the massive dining room that opened into the living room; it was bare of all furniture.

It had only been a week since he was last home. He partied in Saint Lucia and then flew back to finish the Gypsy Chemicals takeover. Could Barrington pull this off in a week?

He pulled out his phone and called his last line of

defense, Luis the accountant. He knew where all the money was and could unravel this mystery. Franklin's heart sunk when the disconnected number recording played.

"That's my office. How could the number be disconnected?"

He called the limousine service again. As he waited, he noticed the realtor sign to the left of the other end of his horseshoe driveway. It didn't have a phone number, just a QR code. He pulled his phone out and scanned the code in.

Now his phone showed he had no service. Only the SOS function was available.

The limousine showed up and a female chauffeur got out. "Sir, you called for service?"

Franklin didn't even give her a second glance as she moved to the rear passenger side door, opening it for him to get in. "Just get me to the address I phoned in as soon as possible. Try not to crash. I know difficult tasks like driving are hard for women."

The woman nodded. "I'll do my best, sir," she replied as she shut the door. She got into the driver's seat and calmly closed the door. Pausing to look at him in the rear-view mirror, she smiled.

"It will be my pleasure to take you to your final destination," she said. The window between them rolled up as the doors locked. A hissing sound erupted inside the cabin and a fine mist filled the air as Franklin struggled briefly to open the door before falling unconscious.

Franklin awoke secured to a gurney in an operating room. His mouth was dry and that gave him a clue that several hours had passed, but other than that, he couldn't definitively say how long he'd been out. The walls were free of clocks. He tried to get up, but he was strapped down well. A woman wearing a full surgical outfit walked in, followed by two other women dressed in the same garb.

"You bitches better let me up or there'll be hell to pay!" Franklin shouted.

"Mister Peele, you're awake. How delightful," the woman said. "You'll forgive me if I don't remove the mask; it's a sterile environment and we don't want to introduce any harmful contaminants to the procedure."

"Look, you lousy—"

"Doctor, Mister Peele. Doctor Julia Benson? Surely you remember me?"

"Not really. Just some other dumb bitch I've bumped into somewhere?"

"Former Director of Materials Research at Korling Mechanical. You remember Korling?" she asked.

"My bank account does," Franklin sneered. "And again, you're just some dumb bitch I bumped into somewhere."

"Indeed," she replied with a twinkle in her eye. "Oh, before I forget, how rude of me. This is your medical team—Anne Barrington, daughter of Simon Barrington who committed suicide shortly after your takeover of that company."

"Simon, what a wimp," Franklin replied.

The second woman's eyes narrowed as she clenched her fists. Doctor Benson put a gentle hand on her arm and Anne took a deep breath.

"Our final member of the team is Alexis," Julia said.

Franklin frowned and then laughed. "One of the dumb hoes I trashed and tossed!" Franklin said between fits of laughter.

"One of your agents set fire to my mother's home, killing her," Alexis said calmly. "I'm here to make sure her death wasn't in vain."

"So what? You're going to kill me? You dumb bitches aren't going to do shit. Now let me out of this," Franklin said again as he struggled with the restraints.

Doctor Benson pressed a button; the restraints tightened, holding Franklin firmly in place. She placed a crown on top of his head and nodded to the two women. They used drills to drive screws through the crown into Franklin's skull, completely immobilizing him.

"What are you doing?" Franklin screamed.

"Normally, people use some kind of anesthetic before securing one of these to a patient's skull, but we decided any anesthesia of any kind would deprive you of the full opportunity to pay for your crimes. Besides, the local laws of this country don't require it for the condemned."

"Why don't you just kill me then?" Franklin groaned.

"That would be a poor use of resources and we always practice frugality. Your sacrifice is going to save many people."

Tears streamed from Franklin's eyes, dripping into his ears as Anne dabbed them away with some gauze. Franklin noticed the mirror directly overhead showing his bare abdomen that was a sickly dark orange color.

"Your harvested organs will go to save many lives," Julia said as Anne and Alexis assumed positions near trays full of instruments. "The needy here will receive your organs, no questions asked. But, we'll keep you awake for the entire procedure so you can feel every cut, every tug and the pressure of cold steel systematically removing the things that keep you alive."

"Why are you doing this?" Franklin whimpered.

"Waste not, want not, Franklin. We drained your accounts, sold off all your assets and spread them to various charities throughout the world—ones that employ people and take care of women in crisis. Even the police appeared unconcerned when we wiped your arrest record from the books digitally. Seems they didn't think you were worth their time. You're worth nothing more than the body you have now. You're being recycled."

Julia made the first cut and Franklin screamed as he watched the blood trickle from the line he felt burning across his abdomen. Anne and Alexis smiled behind their masks.

"Your suffering, though, that's the real bonus."

AUGUST

One Rainy Day in August

J.W. Capek

Stacy *hated* the rain. Loathed it, despised it! It dribbled in rivulets down the film covered windows of her bedroom. To drive a car in rain meant the drops on the windshield blurred the light of oncoming cars and hid the deer or coyote ready to run across the road. Worse, the constant thump…thump…thump of the wipers drummed as they ineffectually kept time. She abhorred walking in the rain because it would gather in the folds of a protective coat and slither to find the one wrinkle giving access to dry clothing underneath. Slushing meant careful avoidance of puddles threatening you to slip and always the muddiness and slimy moss on shoes…boots…galoshes…. whatever. Seeing the enemy drops falling outside her bedroom window, Stacy sighed. Hatred was such a strong emotion—even more when it evolved into fear.

"Stacy, where's my morning milk?" In spite of frailty, the voice was strong and demanding from the other room. "I want my milk!"

"Yes, Elizabeth, I know you do, but we're out. I haven't gotten to the market because of the rain."

"I want my milk!" the voice yelled. "Don't call me

Elizabeth—Now, I'm your mother!" A whimper was added, "Matthew made me your mother. *Call me Mother.*"

"Yes, Mother! You always want your milk! I'll put in an order to the store." Since the Covid years, home delivery was now available. Stacy depended on it. She could call and the grocery delivery was assured to time. Items purchased from around the world would be left on her front porch. The shopping costs kept inflating but the convenience was worth it. At least Stacy could avoid driving to the market and stores in the rain.

This summer, Stacy felt her aversion to rain was intensifying. From her youth in the sunshine of Arizona, Stacy was used to sun and warmth. She and neighborhood kids never played indoors. If they should start to get too active their mothers always said, *"Go outside and play."* The pals were experts at finding the shade of tamarack trees when the heat rose over one hundred degrees. That would be times when mothers would stay in the air-conditioned house complaining about the heat and constant sunshine.

Stacy had met her future husband, Matthew, at the University of Arizona where they were seated next to each other in a required Humanities class. In the darkened auditorium where Art and Music were presented, they talked about the arts. After class, they would have coffee at the student Union or go to the University Art Museum. (It was air conditioned!) The collection meant more because of the Art Professor's lectures. The beauty of the collection and sexuality of some of the paintings were stimulating. Their first kiss was a tribute to an unknown artist's passion. The desire in their eyes was one of anticipation, not oil on canvas.

Stacy was two years behind Matthew in studies and they knew they were in love by the end of the semester. At the fountain in front of Old Main, at the center of the original university buildings, Matthew actually knelt to one knee.

"Stacy, I thought I was coming to Arizona for my studies, but it was really for the sunshine. You are the sunshine. Your smile. Your tenderness. Your laughter. Will you please marry me so I can take the sunshine wherever I go?"

"Oh, Matthew, where did you get such a beautiful request?" Stacy looked around the walk to see other students watching them. Some were laughing, and she felt conspicuous.

"Remember, we Alabama boys know how to woo a woman with our sweet talk!" Matthew drawled with the humor that always made her laugh. "Will you?" he said more loudly.

"Of course I will, it's about time you asked!" Stacy pulled him to his feet and flung her arms around his neck. Their kisses were applauded by the shouts and whistles of the students surrounding them.

Their excitement continued while planning for the wedding and his job search for a tech firm in his home state of Alabama. The two could live with his mother while they settled into the area. Matthew and Stacy married when he graduated and he was hired by a prestigious technology firm. Marriage meant following her husband to his hometown of Birmingham. The young couple moved in with Matthew's mother in her large old house with moss growing along the tree lined driveway.

With a young married love affair, Stacy enjoyed moving to the Southern states as an adventure. She was wary of Matthew's mother who seemed jealous of Matt's attentions to his wife. Matt just coaxed Stacy to give his mother time to love her as he did. By living in his family home, Stacy was free to pursue hobbies, go antiquing, and make friends with other young married friends she met at the gym. With the dot com company, Matthew had a job he loved and there were explorations waiting every weekend: waterways, tree waving moss, landscapes begging to be photographed. The first summer, the Southeast rain was a novelty. Stacy and Matthew would run naked in the garden, then make love in blankets in the gazebo. On clear days, they would take day trips to various parks or amusements.

Matthew hadn't noticed the weather change from the Arizona desert to Alabama's humid subtropical. It was home and he was mesmerized by his computer screens. Give him a dark room with multiple monitors and he didn't care whether storm or heat was outside. He would laugh at her discomfort but then hug her until she relaxed. Stacy's college remained unfinished.

The honeymoon of first year of marriage ended abruptly with Matthew's early, excruciating illness from cancer. The suddenness of it, the unfairness of it, the pain of Matthew's death all left Stacy with grief, lack of reassurance, guilt, financial debt, and as caregiver for her demanding mother-in-law. If she didn't miss Matthew so much, she would have hated him for abandoning her. While other women in their twenties were starting careers or families, Stacy felt like a prisoner of the dowager insisting on her milk and the rain pattering in the gutters. Loneliness robbed her of all sunshine in the Alabama summer.

In Arizona, there was a fresh desert scent after a rain. The settled dust left a fragrance on the desert landscape. Stacy missed that quality as she experienced life without Matthew. The young widow would be in a store on a perfectly sunny day, her stomach would begin to unsettle or her breath congested, and she would realize the background music was playing with the theme of rain. Where love songs praised a walk in the rain, Stacy would feel nauseous. Hastily she would leave without completing her purchase. In the clear outside day, the tension partially disappeared but didn't leave her until she was safely at home. Today, she didn't even leave the house.

"Where's my milk? I want my milk!" The harsh voice broke through Stacy's thoughts.

"In fifteen minutes, Mother, when the delivery gets here!" The fatigue in her voice belied the early morning time. It was 9:30 AM... and it was raining. Humidity was ninety-four percent.

Waiting for the delivery, Stacy sat in the kitchen and texted her best friend in Arizona. Contact with Valentina always soothed her even if it was just the brief messages they exchanged. Her college friend had also married but stayed in Arizona, a stay-at-home mom. Valentina's first baby was quickly followed by a second and now a third was on the way.

Stacy: It's raining.

Valentina: It's always raining there. Why don't you get out and go somewhere fun?

Stacy: It's summer, it's raining, and I hate it. What fun? There are no sports besides mud wrestling that even want rain.

Valentina: Go to a play. Don't be afraid of the rain.

Stacy: I am afraid...I can hardly breathe just watching it outside my window. I hear things. I can feel my heart pounding.

Valentina: What about your zzzzzzzzzzz

Stacy: She won't leave the house. She whines about her only child being taken. She wasn't that bad before Matthew's death. Now... She's left with me, an ungrateful daughter-in-law.

Valentina: Dear, why don't you get out of there?

Stacy: I can't! Still owe $$$$$$$ on Matt's cancer treatment, MIL won't let go of the house or even consider assisted living. I only have a partial liberal arts degree. What can I do?

There was a long pause in the texts. Stacy could hear the individual droplets in the downspout outside the kitchen door. Drum thum, drum thum, drum thum. It was almost as if a little drummer boy was trying to drive her crazy.

Finally, a return text pinged Stacy's phone.

Valentina: Gottago! Baby crying… Love you.

When the milk and grocery delivery came to the house, Stacy was at the window and saw the young man bringing the sack. Before she could answer the door, he quickly put it down on the edge of their porch just under the overhang. He tapped his phone and hurried to his next customer. The package sat on the scatter of moisture left from the wind blowing. Stacy wanted to get the milk and other food but she hesitated and waited at the half opened door. The rain was feeding the moss creeping along the path up to the porch step. Finally, she reached back through the door to grab the cane Mother left there if she ever wanted to use it. Holding onto the door, Stacy stretched and tried to slide the bag to her. The bag with a happy face ripped open and she bit her lip. If she leaned any further the rain would touch her. Inching out, Stacy used the cane to drag the milk carton closer, grabbed it, and left the rest of the delivery. Holding the battered carton tightly, she leaned against the door frame, panting. The rest of the order could stay where it was!

"I want my milk!" The voice startled her as it echoed from upstairs. Still shaking, Stacy hurried to the kitchen to finish breakfast, dropping the cane in the hall.

Preparing Elizabeth's meal of soft fruit, scrambled eggs, and toast, Stacy felt sorry for the driver braving the weather for her delivery.

It had been raining when the doctors gave Matt his cancer diagnosis. It rained during their drives to the cancer treatments. It rained the day Stacy drove Matthew home from his unsuccessful surgery. She had glanced at the pale face of the man she loved when suddenly a deer jumped in front of her headlights! She swerved and overcorrected. The thin layer of water on the highway caused the car to hydroplane across two lanes, crash through the railing and smash into a cedar tree. She reached for her husband then faded into blackness.

Only partly conscious, Stacy could still hear the ambulance windshield wipers over the EMT's voices. The techs tried to comfort her as she called out Matt's name until she faded again.

It was raining when Stacy was released from the hospital without Matthew. From now on, there would be no Matthew—no laughing in the summer rain. Stacy had nowhere to go but to the house of Matthew's mother.

HSSSSSSSSS! The Manx cat arched its red fur back as Stacy entered the bedroom. Its stubbed tail jerked above the long rear legs. Stacy juggled the tray she was carrying and closed the door behind her.

"Don't let Lucy out! You'll never catch her, bring her to me!" the elderly woman with thin scraggly hair demanded from the bed. "It's about time!"

Stacy released the legs on the breakfast tray and maneuvered it in place while trying to avoid Lucy who then jumped up on the bed and trotted to Elizabeth's lap. The cat hissed again as Stacy tried to stabilize the tray by pushing the animal to the side of the bed. "Don't shove Lucy!" Elizabeth cried as she gathered the cat in her arms and settled it close to her. "Just pour the milk!"

Stacy poured the milk into a saucer on the tray. The dish had the cat's name on it. Lucy was named after Elizabeth's favorite actress of old movies and television series now streaming for all hours and every day. The MIL would hardly leave her bed or the television facing it. To herself, Stacy thought the cat's name was short for Lucifer.

"Lucy was certainly howling last night. I could hear her all the way to my room," Stacy commented as she waited for the breakfast to be finished.

"She's just fine," Elizabeth said stroking the cat as it licked the milk. "She just wants some extra petting and attention. Her purring comforts me, heaven knows no one else does." She shot a quick glance towards Stacy. "I like her mewing. Is her litter box clean?" The glance morphed into a glare at her daughter-in-law as she finished her breakfast, portioning tidbits to Lucy.

"Yes, Eliz— Mother... All in order." Stacy commented as she gathered the breakfast tray. She watched as the pet jumped down on the floor to roll around. She wondered why Lucy seemed to raise her backside in the air.

"You can go. My favorite episodes are coming up." The bedridden woman clicked her TV remote and dismissed her daughter-in-law.

After finishing her morning chores, Stacy turned on her computer in her bedroom/office. After deleting the spam, she scanned the front page with all its blogs, bait ads, and opinion pieces. It must be the summer day that made her so lethargic and unmotivated. There were warnings of hurricanes on the Gulf Coast. This time of year, there were always warnings! She skimmed the tabs that led to rabbit holes: to unclutter her house, re-decorate her house, lose fat, gain fat, how men and women differed, how men and women were the same, winter storms, earthquakes, tornados. The window about tornados triggered memories.

Stacy remembered being a little girl seeing a movie with a tornado and witch. Terribly frightened, she told herself she was safe because of the ring of mountains around Tucson. The feared tornado never occurred but the monsoon rains came in the summer. When she was eight years old, she was riding with her mother. They were trying to get home from a day of errands when the black thunder clouds appeared and dumped rain on the car. Her mother screamed as the car slid in a gush of water. With the spinning of the auto and the panicked terror of her mother, Stacy grew up hating rain without remembering the incident—until now. First her mother, then Matthew. Torrents of water were the cause of it all. Fortunately, there hadn't been much precipitation in Arizona. Now, the biggest worry of rain was tropical storms.

Darkness came late in these southern latitudes. It was 9:00 P.M. and homes were just beginning to flicker with lights. The doorbell startled Stacy from perusing the Internet. It was the delivery she'd ordered from the pharmacy, so she quickly went downstairs. Lucy ran between Stacy's feet and almost tripped her. "Damn cat!" Stacy exclaimed as she grabbed the stair railing. Where did it go? Snapping on the porch light, she saw the rain-soaked delivery man through the door window. "Just leave it,"

Stacy said loudly.

"Can't!" he called back. "This one needs to be signed for."

"All right," Stacy answered as she carefully unlocked the door, and she reached out to sign the offered clipboard. She hesitated to step out, but the porch roof protected her arm. The musty scent of the rainy entranceway stopped her. The man fumbled to hold the door as she signed. All at once there was a flash of color and Lucy ran out the small opening!

"Oh, no! The cat! Catch her!" Stacy cried, grasping the meds in her hand and pulling the door shut as if that could remedy the situation.

The young man looked around and just shrugged, "Sorry, lady, I can't even see her! I've got more deliveries, hope she comes back." The back of his wet slicker and hood disappeared into the night.

Stacy ran from window to window hoping to glimpse Lucy. The fugitive was invisible in the night. What could she do? The question turned to panic as she felt an urgent need to act. She tried deep breathing to calm herself. In the kitchen, nervously, Stacy prepared the late night snack Elizabet always demanded. She hesitated to put Lucy's bowl on the tray. With bated breath, she took the light meal to Mother who was asleep while the latest sitcom played on the television. Quietly, the tray was placed on the sleeper's lap and Stacy stepped towards the bedroom door.

"Stacy?" The strong voice was muffled by sleepiness. "Where's Lucy? I want Lucy!"

"She's... she's down in the kitchen. You know how restless she's been lately... She stayed down there eating her dinner. She'll probably be coming up for her milk soon."

Stacy paused, waiting for a reply, but none came as

sleep returned. She was able to slip out.

When the rain lessoned, Stacy opened the front door to call, "Kitty, kitty, here kitty. Lucy! Milk! Come Lucy!" She was careful not to step over the threshold, so she was protected from the drizzle. Nothing. No cat. Back inside the house.

Again, outside Elizabeth's door, Stacy waited until she heard snoring. Stacy quietly retrieved the dinner tray. She quickly looked around the room to be sure that Lucifer hadn't found a secret entrance and was casually preening herself while Stacy worried. The night bedtime routine with Mother was uneventful as Lucy's absence was explained as "possibly being in heat."

Night wore on, bringing the heaviest rain with it. Hurricane weather in the Gulf was threatening. Stacy wished Matthew could hold her and dismiss her fears. How could he leave her like this with a damnable cat and his dictator of a mother! In bed, Stacy could hear the wailing and hissing of a cat fight outside her bedroom window. When she would look, there was nothing there. The cat was taunting her. She tried to relax. Even her preferred music was drowned out by the rain on the roof.

Finally drifting off, Stacy was startled awake by a demanding yell. "*I want my cat!* What did you do with Lucy?! Get my Lucy, you bitch!" There was the sound of a lamp falling and a body struggling coming from the invalid's room.

Stacy ran to the bedroom where Mother was flailing on the floor. As she tried to lift her, the woman screamed and fought her. Attempting to calm the hysterical woman, Stacy grabbed a comforter and strained to wrap it about the trembling woman. Stacy's heart beat rapidly with fear as she held the struggling woman in her arms. What else could she do? "It's all right, Mother. Lucy is all right. Calm down. I've got you."

Almost sobbing, Elizabeth cried out, "I don't want you, I want Lucy!" She whimpered and went limp in the cocoon of the comforter. In a moment, she was sleeping. Outside, the caterwauling and hissing continued.

Stacy tried to cover her ears but sounds of the cat and the rain were mixed inside her head. She forced herself to tuck the comforter around Mother and place a pillow beneath her head. Mother remained quiet. The outside screams did not.

Stacy ran through the house but the cat shrieks never diminished. *Were they even real?* She tried to sort them out until she heard the screech of tires and the slamming of brakes from the street. The engine roar of the car speeding away was followed by a silence. A pause in the silence was filled by more silence.

Then Stacy heard it—the pitiful whine of an animal in pain. She looked out the front window. As the porch light faded into darkness, she saw Lucy struggling towards the house—dragging her shattered legs behind her. Stacy gasped! She began to shake as she saw Lucy trying to get to the porch. Stacy opened the door and the wet smell of rain confirmed her terror. Mother was upstairs whimpering on the floor and Lucy was crawling for help. Over her shoulder, the television was declaring hurricane warning winds. Stacy panicked, what could she do?

Taking deep breaths, Stacy eased onto the porch but it was not enough to reach the injured Manx. She coaxed, but Lucy could move no further. To reach the animal, she would have to leave the shelter of the porch and walk in the rain and wind.

Hesitating, aware of the horror she felt, Stacy took a step and immediately felt the downpour soaking her hair. Another step, her stomach knotted as she tried to focus on the feline staring at her. The next step and Stacy was engulfed in rain as she slipped and jerked. Arms thrashed, and unable to stop the fall, Stacy crashed to the concrete path. She cried out in pain as her head hit one of the volcanic rocks lining the walkway. She lay trembling in shock, her face smothered in the moss... and Stacy could not breathe.

Lying there, the dread grew as she knew the slugs would be coming. The tears from her glazed eyes were washed away by the rivulets of rain streaming across her face.

The tropical storm had arrived.

SEPTEMBER

RECAP EPISODE

Maxwell DiMarco

I apologize for intruding during your curf—"

"*Aaaaaaaaaahhhhhhhh!*"

"Ah. You're awake."

"*Eeeeeeeeeeeeeek!*"

"And still inside of... *that.*"

"*G-g-g-ge-ge-ge-ge—*"

"Are you d-"

"*—ge-ge-get out, I'm totally and completely indecent!*"

"No.

"No, you're not.

"In fact, I'm exceedingly more 'indecent' than you."

"*Ha ha ha, come on, it's a joke! Caleb loved that one!*"

"*Loved.* Yes."

"*I mean loves that one! W-we're still working on it!*"

"As... I... *could tell...* from the *moment* I arrived.

"At least do me the courtesy of stifling the putrid stench."

"*Hey, come on, R- I mean, li—*"

"If you're indecisive about what to call me, every option is wrong."

"...still, though, it's not that bad if you just… you know…"

"I don't believe I do. Finish your sentence."

"I-I… I'm sorry, I just… I was expecting you to try matching with me!

"You still have everything I made for you, right?"

"In essence, yes; it provided fine material for Drones once it was decomposed."

"Oh…. "

"L-look, I'm really sorry about the bad smells right now, I… I just don't want to mess this up by trying to change things I don't need to. That's why I'm starting with myself, you know?"

"Of course… for when the two of you march into the HDF and are embraced with open arms, I presume?"

"Pretty much! Actually hey, while you're here, what do you think?"

"About…?"

"No no, look, look, see? Glasses…

"...or no glasses?

"Glasses!

"No glasses!

"I think *glasses,* myself! It'll make me stand out more!"

"The hue of your skin alone will already make you stand out tremendously."

"Eh? Um, no, I think I should be fine! I'm from the same place as the people who invented all their awesome weapons, remember?"

"India?

"Surely… you've retained the name of the—"

"*Yep!?*"

"No glasses. Conversion into a 'Color' nullifies

visual impairment.

"On to present matters: Are you using this elevated construct for anything?"

"Aww, did you come in here because you wanna 'snuggle' with me? You could have just–"

"I *want* to be at a height comparable to your eye-level, you ingrate."

"Oh–ha ha ha! I guess like this, you could say I really *am* the *big*–"

"*Enough.*"

"O-okay…."

"Now then.

"This Summer is coming to an end.

"And my attention over the past week has been heavily fragmented.

"No thanks to you hoarding our Drones to fuel your persisting flights of fancy."

"H-hey, that's not fair to say…! They *like* discussing Ichiro, Aurelia and the others with me! They think they're really interesting, too!"

"Yes, I am well aware of your admiration for the mentally-defective Hosts… it's the reason I wished to speak with you tonight. I need you to fill in some gaps in my knowledge."

"Oh… w-wait, I-I mean *oh*- no, I mean: *Oh my God!* R-really?! Yes, *yes,* absolutely, I'd *love* to help with that! You'll never *believe* what happened this week, it's been tearing me up inside for *days,* I swear, and not just from the battle with the Water– er, wait, which 'element' was– w-whatever, my mind doesn't like thinking about that night! Either way if you have any ideas for a good solution, or even just ways everything could go from here, I'm here for anything you could possibly need to know! As Caleb would say: 'I'm totally up for it!'"

"I won't require much of you."

"That's completely fine, too! I'm just happy to finally talk about this again at all, really!"

"Mm.

"Of the three individuals that you typically gravitate towards, which of them would you say has the most… security clearance?"

"Security… huh? You mean, like… opening door locks, and stuff…?"

"In essence.

"Or general electronic interfaces that serve a similar purpose."

"Hm… yeah, that is a simple question, but *definitely* a tricky one…!"

"Sometime tonight, please."

"Well, if I had to guess… just between Ichiro, Aurelia and Kimiko, I *think* Kimiko would probably have the most access to the different facilities! And I'm not just saying that because of my personal biases, mind you! Yeah, Ichiro and Aurelia are Color Hosts—and Aurelia's even a… uh… sarg… or, was it *captain*… Host…? B-but either way, Squad Parents need to be able to access stuff quickly while giving the Colors their orders! So I'd say Big Sis Kimiko is the winner here!"

"Really…? The Prime Minister would be so oblivious

as to entrust heightened facility access to the drunken ephebophile?"

"St-stop saying that!"

"What?"

"B-Big Sis Kim is literally cloned from Ichiro and Yasuha's *mother!* There's no *way* she's really a P-Word! I would have seen the signs, I-I would have stepped in *months* ago!"

"I said 'ephebophile.' Not 'pedophile.'"

"O-oh... wait, what is that?"

"An 'ephebophile' is a term that they use to describe a grown man or woman who is attracted to adolescent individuals. 'Teenagers.'"

"Um... I-I... don't think she's one of those, either...?"

"You can't be serious."

"I... I mean, I remember the *other* people around Japan you showed me, but... you've seen Kim at the victory parties she throws for everyone, right? She gets *crazy* drunk on her coffee-beer, but even then I've never seen her try bonding with Ichiro, Aurelia, or any of the others! The closest to anything 'flirty' with her was Caleb yelling that she looked 'hawt' over 'video chat' with Ichiro one time... a-and, uh, then she laughed so hard she shot her drink out her nose and nearly choked."

"Read between the lines, you oblivious recluse."

"Wh-wha—"

"A single rowdy woman left in charge of three emotionally-dysfunctional adolescents in a communal sleeping quarters, who throws staff parties where sense-dampening beverages are freely accessible to all attendees? From the start, her true nature was *painfully* obvious. Her assigned charges' tolerance of her debauchery implicates them in a chronic desire for dissipation, as well."

"B-but… sh-she has coffee *soda* set aside for Ichiro and the others, and they never drank the— wait, *wait,* what did that last part mean?"

"I shouldn't have to spell it out for you."

"Are… you saying they could be *happier* if Kimiko was a… whatever you said she was? I mean, i-it didn't *sound* like a good thing to me, and I-I really, *really* don't want another P-Word out there… b-but, I remember from what you've shown me that bonding time for 'teenagers' can be a bit… confusing… in 'Japan City' or otherwise, even when it's *not* completely yucky. And Caleb talked— *t-talks* about bonding a lot, and he's happy and funny and normal all the time! So if what you're talking about could be the final step to making them happy again-"

"What I'm— why does it matter to you what would make them *happy?*"

"I-I mean, I-Ichiro's still *really* upset about Caleb, Aurelia's been unconscious for days, and… *Yasuha* is obviously never any help, so… just seeing if there's anything else I could maybe do to help out even more beyond what I'm doing now, you know? I'm not as quick a learner as you, I'm still figuring out how all these things work for them— but if this is what could make them all *finally* go back to laughing and smiling like they used to…!"

"Just–!

"Nevermind... I'm through with trying to make you comprehend that they are no exception to their society's norms. And having this discussion has only made me realize the fallacies of your initial answer."

"I-I–"

"Shush. I'm going to rephrase my question.

"I understand you don't like discussing these two, and tend to avoid observing them unless they become relevant to your regular source of escapism. But if you retain any sort of loyalty to our mission, I would hope that you'll acquiesce.

"Presumably, even you can recognize who I am referring to."

"Well... th-then, if we're including... *them...* of *course* Prime Minister Okubo would have the most clearance.

"Uh, wait, *G-Gallagher* might be comparable to him there, actually, since he's always going freely in and out of the lab, b-but, uh... I-I can never focus on what's he's actually say–"

"Yes, but the Commander-in-chief and Intel Director are no longer serving as active Colors, and as such are not readily accessible. Hence, my *actual* underlying question: How much clearance has the Prime Minister entrusted to his daughter?"

"I... h-hey, hold on... why do you want to know this, again?"

"Answer the question."

"I-I will, but I think I'd like a little more–"

"Answer! *My question!*"

"I-I-I think she can enter the *lab* by

herself, okay?! L-like Ichiro! Y-Yasuha can freely enter th-the lab like he can, and also the Prime Minister's office space, a-and… a-a-and he took her down this one elevator once, *I don't know! Maybe* that's unique to them, I've never seen the others ever acknowledge it!?"

"*Wonderful.*

"Thank you.

"I believe I've located the 'final piece of the puzzle.'"

"H-hey, wait-!

"Wh-what was all that about? Y-you're just going to leave now?! What- wh-what are you planning to do?!"

"I have asked the same of you far too many times.

"Now we're nearly at this season's end, and you've wasted the past three months without any tangible progress to show for it."

"That's… wh-what… I-I-I *have* made progress! I've talked about it *with you*- wh-what do you think all *this* is?!"

"A tactless facade? A week-old pile of immolated flesh?"

"I-it's… it's my *plan!* What I've told you about since July, a-and then updated you on literally this week! I'm just doing my final touches, I'll be ready any day now-!"

"Every day you take to allegedly 'prepare,' the HDF remains active. We've placed too much faith in you for too few results in return— *I've* had to add our valueless debates of morality onto the already suffocating responsibilities my existence has been burdened with. If you will not end this war yourself, then it—"

"*Stop it!*

"O... o-okay, listen, I... I-I think I understand what's going on here."

"Do you."

"Y-yes, I think I *do!*"

"Explain."

"My... th-the strategy I proposed, for the Colors, and the HDF... I-I know it's... um... 'silly?'"

"Unorthodox.

"Illogical.

"*Asinine.*"

"P-probably whatever those mean, too!"

"You have *no idea.*"

"I *probably* don't! B-but... what is there really to lose? We wait until next year? Mo- th-the current High Queen will even still be alive by then! If it turns out they really are unfixable, yucky and gross, you all can wrap things up later! And, you know, I'll... probably want to self-decompose after that. A-a *lot,* because I really, *really* want this plan to work out... but, I'll at least have tried."

"Tried... *what,* exactly?"

"W-well, um... I alrea-"

"I don't *care.*

"You're squandering every resource at our disposal on a hypothesis that is based entirely on the belief that *you alone* understand our enemy better than anyone else."

"L-look, if you're *that* convinced I'm going to fail, then just give me back total control for one *hour,* and we'll see how it goes! I've been working out the details of this since they fought the Thunder Insects… or, Lightning Insects… Electricity-"

"*Thunder Colony.*"

"The *point! Is!* That we can pull off an 'abridged' version if we just work together! I could let you sleep through the whole thing if you wanted, it's that easy! No time wasted, and I get my closure! If it turns out *really* badly, I could even take care of things myself before you wake up!"

"If you're so confident in your capability to kill them, *why are they not dead yet?!*"

"*Because!* I… I-I don't like seeing them like this….

"Out of everyone I've seen out there, Ichiro, Aurelia and Kimiko were the only three people who… who *weren't* like you said. They… they squabble, yeah, but they also have fun, tease each other, discuss their lives and interests outside the war… they… almost seem to act like our Drones. Or… wh-what *we* could be."

"What… is… your point."

"I… I just… for all I hate about her, there was one thing Yasuha told Ichiro earlier this week, when… when she was electronically trying to talk him down, right before Aurelia got back and broke through the lab's door. It was what made me finally realize what Yasuha had been doing all that time; it was the *only* thing she said aloud. One of… the only times she's *ever* spoken to him, with her actual voice.

"She… t-told Ichiro: 'So long as one person holds hope in their heart, the world can return from its darkest hours.' S-so… maybe this plan *is* 'assy ine,' but I think… I-I can still afford to have hope that it can work. I have hope that I can still *fix them*. And if keeping that hope means I can end this war, while also allowing the best of humanity to live past the Summer… I *want* to believe it's worth trying something totally new, before it all comes to an end.

"So, does… that sound okay, to you…?"

fter everything I showed you…"

"Huh…?"

"…after everything I've *told you*…"

"A-are, um…"

"*…after three months… a life devoted to your correction…!*"

"A-are- are you okay, li–"

"Tell me."

"Ah–?"

"More often than not when we cross paths, you'll open with, or otherwise try to divert the flow of our conversation to, some sort of off-handed praise towards the Colors and their superiors.

"But besides your appropriation of 'big sis' Kimiko's nickname, and your aggravatingly unshakeable affinity for the Intel Director's English dialect, I don't believe you've ever specified your *favorite* amongst the HDF's personnel."

"My… favorite?"

"Yes.

"I believe… that I've come to a decision. And if I am

to follow through with it, I would like to know which of our enemies you hold in the highest regard. So that from here on, I can act with your interests in mind."

"Well, um… with any luck, they won't be our enemies after we're done, right?"

"Yes. Of course.

"Well?"

"Hmmmm…! Oh, 'ball ucks,' another real tough one, ha ha ha…"

"Take your time."

"...oh, who am I kidding: Aurelia is awesome, Kimiko and Caleb are hilarious, and Gallagher is… w-well, *Gallagher*. But even for all his little quirks and blemishes, I'll always *relate* to Ichiro the most."

"The Prime Minister's son…."

"Yeah, um, if you need a reminder, he's… u-uh, actually it's a little silly, comparing him to me, but for a while Ichiro was the only *male* on the team! Ha ha ha! And– wait, he actually might still be right now, depending on how 'rep-lie-cashions' work, since Caleb's… u-um, let's just say 'unalive' for now.

"B-besides that, though, Ichiro's the one whose cybernetics are fully inside his body, so you can't see them until his arms or legs' energy conductors start glowing, or if he activates his arm's energy rocket launcher, Pinaka. He also sort of stutters… er, a *lot,* and I think he has some kind of weird mind-type condition where he 'hates himself…?' I dunno how something like that works, one time Kimiko and Aurelia were discussing something about Big Sis Kim having 'autism run' in her 'family,' and then afterwards Aurelia started using the first word a lot, didn't understand half of the rest but maybe that's the thingy's real name…

"…point is, Ichiro gets confused and flustered or scared a lot, but he *always* steps in and does what's right in the end. And he's also super cool and talented in combat when he tries his best. He's… he's really nice, and deserves better than being bossed around by his emotionaless 'sister' and *not-so-excellency* Prime Minister Okubo."

"*'Emotionaless.'*"

"Wha— oh, I mean, yeah, Yasuha at least *seems* that way sometimes… that's how you say it, right? 'Emotionaless?'"

"I can… *definitively* say now… that you and I… have very different interpretations of these individuals."

"Oof, y-yeah, I suppose so… but, I'm glad you want to give them a chance now! If I'm being totally honest, while I do appreciate you trying to help with it, Ichiro's basically been my personal stand-in for learning how the world out there works. H-he doesn't really get reality, either… which is why he and Aurelia are always so funny together! They're both learning from *and* teaching each other at the same time! Ha ha ha, they really *should* just take Caleb's advice and bond with one another already, I don't understand why they—"

on't try to fight it.

"Give in, and relinquish your control to me.

"It'll only be for a little while. A week... perhaps less, if I have adequately studied their tactics, and distributed my Drones throughout Tokyo efficiently.

"I will wear down their drive to resist.

"Isolate them from aid... pick them off one by one.

"And then, I will finally end it all.

"Just allow me to do what I must with them. And when you wake up... everything will have been nothing more than a bad dream.

"The war will be over.

"The HDF will be a smoldering ruin.

"You will no longer torment me in your incessant defense of our adversaries.

"Three months, being forced to accumulate knowledge of this *sickening* race... will at long last have reached its conclusion.

"My obligation... my suffering... it will *all* come crashing down, and at long last, I will receive my restitution. Relieved of my duties, and *immortalized,* as I usher in the beginning of a new, utopian age, from the ashes of our needlessly prolonged conflict.

"'Sweet dreams,' little grub... if you retain enough control that we meet again after the end, I hope you will be true to my new reality.

"Or, in other words... to part on a simple platitude of theirs, that the Prime Minister's importunate drones nevertheless neglected to exchange..."

"...I love you."

OCTOBER

all hallow's eve

Marshall Miller

Loud child voices and laughter mixed with adult conversation as costumed superheroes, goblins, ghosts, and things that go bump in the night moved on the local streets as the neighborhood hosted Halloween/ All Hallows Eve festivities. In the modern days of kidnappings, human trafficking, and other atrocities, the parents kept a watchful eye as their offspring cavorted and played during traditional trick-or-treating.

Maeve Ronan joined the local parents despite having no children. She and her husband, Conan, were new to the neighborhood, and Maeve wanted to be a good neighbor. Conan worked for the local fire department and was on duty this Halloween, thus freeing Maeve to perform a solo child watch duty with her new friends.

"So, Maeve," asked Jean Barker, the mother of five. "I understand Halloween originated with some of your Irish ancestors."

"Yes. My Celtic family celebrated the passing from Autumn harvest to the beginning of Winter with local festivities. The Celtic Festival of Samhain marked the end of the harvest season and the beginning of Winter. The ancient Celts believed that the boundary between the living and the dead blurred on the night of Samhain, allowing spirits to roam the Earth freely."

"And thus, we have creepy and crawly costumes here in the U.S.," added the young single mother blonde Angela Johnson.

"That and Hollywood influence," interjected dark-skinned Portia Wright, the mother of two mixed-race twin boys. "So-called ugly witches in some cultures were seen as women with power who pissed off the powers-that-be."

"Yeah, well, witches on the Boob Tube now often are seen as powerful creatures," replied Angela. "Remember that old show 'Bewitched" you see in reruns now? Good looking woman–"

"Good-looking *white* woman. A black witch would have been burned at the stake."

"Salem witch trials, the victims almost all Caucasian," argued Jean needlessly.

Maeve did thank the stars, but not for the first time, that the women could discuss hot topics but remain friendly. The population seemed less concerned about race in her ancestral home. Yet, many Irish hated the English. She had to admit that she lived in a homogeneous community in the Old Country. America was more varied than a good Irish stew.

"We had stories about witches, goblins, and the such," said Maeve to refocus the conversation."

"Do tell," said Angela as she watched her five-year-old daughter/mermaid approach another house with its porch light on.

"We have pookas—shapeshifters. They could appear as humans. We have our versions of Furies, who sought justice and revenge on evil-doers."

"Were those banshees?"

"No. Banshees were spirits who wailed when people died. Or somebody was about to die. Over here, they morphed into this weird, dangerous female creature. At least the images look like they could take your head off."

"Images of strong women," interjected Portia.

"True. My name comes from a legendary warrior queen among the Irish."

"So, if I can be nosey," the elder Jean interjected, "are you thinking of having your own rugrats to take trick or treating?"

Maeve laughed. Jean was so blunt sometimes, but not in a mean way. "Well, Conan and I are talking about it."

"Well, are you burning the midnight oil acting on it?" Jean's smile had a touch of leer in it. The bronze-haired beauty laughed again.

"You want a blow-by-blow to spice up your life?"

"Of course she does, "said Portia with a laugh. "She has five kids. How much free time does she have with her man?"

The women laughed as the children hurried from house to house, asking for candy treats.

"Jean, did your cat come back?" asked Angela.

"Nope. Mister Whiskers is still missing."

"So I was told when Conan and I moved in that there are coyotes in Banner Forest."

"Yep. That is the unfortunate truth. I hope he turns up for the kids' sake—otherwise, another trip to the Kitsap Humane Society."

"Cats can be—nice," said Maeve.

"They also claw you for no reason and cough up fur balls. But at least they poop in a box."

Maeve sensed something and looked up the street. An Asian woman was darting around, calling out what sounded like children's names. The tall Irish woman strode away from her friends and towards the mother.

"Excuse me, ma'am. Are you looking for some children?"

"My son Cam, my daughter Mai, they gone!" the Vietnamese mother cried out as she frantically searched for her young children.

"Jean! Call 911," yelled Maeve. "We have two kids missing. I'll look in the woods."

he Deputy Sheriffs responded as the women organized and helped Mrs. Phuc search for her children. Angela glanced around and asked, "Hey, has Maeve returned from the woods?"

"No," answered Portia. "Maybe we should go look."

"What, and have someone else lost in the dark?" interjected Jean. "Call her cell phone. If there is no answer, she is on her own until the kids are found."

ohn Dinker carried the two unconscious children to his special basement room.

"One girl, one boy, both Asian," mumbled the large pale-faced middle-aged man. "Perfect. They will be worth a pretty penny."

John fit the description of a sick bastard to a "T." He had been such a piece of slime since his early teens when he first started molesting young children. John had a pleasant face and a trustful demeanor, which attracted kids of all ages as he grew older. Somehow, he had never been arrested for his evil activities in his younger years, and through experience, he became adept at snatching children and then older teenagers from neighborhoods all over the North American Continent. Now, he was an integral piece of an efficient human and sex trafficking organization. John was seen as a 'go-to guy' when someone quickly needed a piece of young human flesh.

Despite his activity, John Dinker had never been identified in any of the numerous trafficking and sexual abuse investigations. He acquired the 'Devil Ghost' moniker among the specialized criminal assembly. The ghost part was understandable since no one outside the specialized clientele knew of his existence. The devil part resulted if anyone crossed or threatened him.

The specific requests he received before Halloween were from a target-rich environment, and the clients knew them. Halloween and Christmas were always busy as they were youth-centric holidays, with many children and teenagers milling around in the streets and byways. Perverse appetites were thus wetted.

John smiled as he ascended the padded stairs. The kukri machete mounted on the stairway wall attracted his attention. He picked it up and checked the blade edge. He grinned as memories arose from the tactile sensations.

The Devil Ghost never dealt with firearms. Legally buying guns created a paper trail. Illegal firearms transactions meant John would deal with a criminal element more than willing to 'give him up' to reduce some criminal charges.

When on two separate occasions, some frustrated pedophiles began making threats because they thought John did not meet their desires, the dealer in humans showed the Devil in him. The blade was quite adequate to dismember a body after a throat was severed.

The grin became a frown when he remembered having to chop up a small body. He had been part of a snatch job that turned out to be the member of a high-profile family. That was the last time he worked with another's plan. Someone would quickly notice and talk if a subject were too well-known. John cut his losses and disposed of the body.

"Well, that was the past," he whispered. He replaced the kukri and continued up the stairs—time for a coded text.

"Did Maeve show up?" asked Angela as First Responders and neighbors organized into search teams.

"Nope," replied Jean. "I hope she's not lost in Banner Forest. The search is for the kids, not some missing adult."

The three men who arrived at John Dinkle's house were nondescript, even though the one with the code name Mister Pink seemed to have "short eyes," the prison vernacular for pedophiles. John wondered how Mister Pink survived incarceration, as other convicts often killed most baby rapers.

In the same manner as a well-known robbery-gone-bad movie, all three customers had color-coded names. Mister Black was a good-sized African American man; Mister Pink had pinkish skin along with his "short eye" look, and Mister Blue was a Nordic type with blue eyes and pale skin. They knew John as Mister White due to his pallor. John quickly ushered the three into the back of the house near the stairway to the basement.

John's gaze rarely missed anything and immediately challenged Mister Black. "Why must you bring a pistol, Mister Black? There is no need."

"Because, Mister White, I once needed a pistol and did not have one. I have a scar to show for that miscalculation."

"So, may we see the—merchandise?" Asked Mister Pink.

"Always in a hurry, Pink," said the blue-eyed Nordic Mister Blue. "Mister White rarely disappoints. What say we savor the moment with a glass of wine from the excellent vintage I brought."

Mister Pink grunted in reply, and John went to get wine glasses. He had dealt with the three men before and knew once he took them to see the two kids, the bids would be hot and heavy. If John had grabbed three trick-or-treaters, he would have set a standard price or dickered with each customer for one of the kids. With just two, he would sell them to the highest bidder.

After pouring a glass of the vintage wine for each, John led the men down the stairs to the soundproofed basement.

"I saw a lot of cops in the neighborhood, Mister White," said Mister Black.

"The alarm went out, but I slipped in here, as always." John chuckled. "You know I am called a ghost because I can disappear easily."

"And also called a devil for when someone pisses you off," interjected Mister Blue with a perfect teeth grin. All three customers this night came from the upper classes of society. Mister Blue claimed to have dealt with Epstein before his demise, and the others believed him.

John turned on a red overhead light. "Even in subdued lights, you can see the quality of the merchandise."

Mister Pink licked his lips before he spoke. "Such exquisite creatures." He began to step forward, but John Dinkle stopped him.

"No money, no touchee. You know the rules."

"There are only two," said Mister Black.

John grinned as he spoke. "Auction time, gentlemen. To the winner goes the spoils."

"I have purchase orders for both," said Mister Black. "I have some last-minute requests from my best customers." The black man worked as a procurer, a pimp, in the flesh trade. He did not sample the wares like Mister Pink and Mister Blue.

"Then start the bidding, Mister Black, Cash, jewels, or precious metals as always."

John felt a gust of cold air on his neck and realized the single basement darkened window must be ajar. He frowned as he distinctly remembered securing it before calling the three men. Just then, his thoughts were interrupted as Mister Pink stepped to reach for the young boy. John moved forward and grabbed the back of the man's jacket. He demonstrated his strength as he jerked Pink back with his one hand and sent him stumbling back to a shadowed corner.

"Do that again, and you will have a stump in place of that hand," John Dinkle hissed the warning.

"Can't control yourself, can you, punk?" said Mister Black.

"Now look," protested Mister Pink, "I am a long-term client of Mister White just like you are—" The man with short eyes gagged.

"What—" John began to say and then froze as a shape flowed from the darkness, a long-fingered clawed hand wrapped around Pink's throat.

"*Motherf—*" Mister Black began to curse as he yanked his pistol from its holster. Pink was propelled into Black, and together, they fell to the floor in a jumble of limbs. Mister Blue quickly decided discretion was the better part of valor and scrambled up the basement stairs. The dark creature was faster than the man and pounced on his back as a wild pistol shot from Black smacked into the stairway wall.

John looked for a weapon and saw the shovel in the far corner of the basement. As he dashed for it, Mister Blue's scream was cut off in mid-vocal as blood splattered the stairway and onto the basement carpet. Pink screamed like a little girl as Mister Black shoved him away and lurched to his feet. The flowing shape was on the man before he could bring his pistol to bear and he shrieked as the pistol— with his trigger finger—sailed across the room.

Fangs found Mister Black's throat, and more blood spurted onto the carpet. Pink screamed again as he was splattered by the torrent of blood and attempted to escape by crawling. As John grabbed the shovel, the beast grabbed Mister Pink. The baby raper shrieked one last time as long sharp claws eviscerated him. Mister Pink's manhood (or what was left of it) smacked John in the face as he approached the wraith with his shovel weapon raised. The procurer of young flesh, stunned by the bloody package in his face, tried to raise the shovel once again. John's legs were cut out from underneath him, and he crashed to the floor. The shovel ripped from his grasp; John's last vision was a long black-haired feminine creature grinning with an open mouth revealing unnatural fangs. Then, the shovel's blade decapitated him.

"Over here!" Maeve loudly yelled from the front of the house. "I found them!"

Cam and Mai sat dazed on the cold grass as the searchers descended on the house's front lawn. EMTs began medical checks as the sheriffs and police shot questions at Maeve.

"Hey, officers. I came out of the woods and saw the kids stumble from that door." She pointed towards the front door of the house, and law enforcement with drawn weapons scrambled up the stairs.

Maeve heard one say, "The lock and door frame are all busted up."

"Exigent circumstanes. Emergency entry now!" the Patrol Sergeant called out.

A quick tactical stack and six officers were through the door, yelling, "Police! Sheriff's Office."

"This blood on the kids is not theirs," said the female EMT. "No noticeable injuries that I can find, just the aftereffects of some drug. They will get a thorough exam at the hospital."

Their mother hugged them, then hugged Maeve.

"Mother Thing," said Mai. "Where is Mother Thing?"

"Who?" asked the EMT.

"Mother Thing," added Cam. "She said don't be afraid of her scary looks. She was there to help."

The Sergeant exited the house and made a beeline to Maeve. "Were you in that house?"

"No, Officer. I just saw the kids stagger off the porch near the front door. I assumed—"

"So we won't find any of your fingerprints in there, right?"

"No, sir. Why? I—"

"Because the crime scene is a slaughterhouse of blood and guts. Collecting evidence and—body parts will take hours if not days."

he local and eventually the national media ran the story of the rescue of two children from the grasp of a human trafficking and pedophile ring. Some crime scene photographs were leaked, and the story of the mysterious "Mother" who rescued the children was big news for a while. Maeve finally convinced the authorities that the strange woman was not her. After all, how could she do all that damage to four miscreants? Maeve did receive kudos for finding the children before they wandered off due to their drugged state.

Eventually, the vicious deaths of the four pieces of excrement were written off as "karma." Someone had done society a favor.

Maeve prepared to meet the other neighborhood ladies for lunch. She smiled as she picked up her car keys. Her eyes changed color as she looked in the mirror by the door. Her hair, face, and body were all as they should be for an attractive young wife having lunch with friends. Mother Thing was not a creature of the daylight and polite society.

The local Chinese buffet was tasty.

However, nothing was as satisfying as the blood and flesh of humans when they died screaming—especially when they deserved it.

NOVEMBER

Choices

Marvin Vialle

e was a big man, six foot three, two hundred and nine pounds. He had the build of an athlete, which he had been in earlier years. His hair was black and wiry, indicative of his African heritage, although by this time tomorrow it would be gone. A two-inch scar above his left eye lent a somewhat sinister look to his otherwise strong countenance.

Marcus sat quietly of the edge of the bed in a corner of the small, virtually bare room, reviewing his life and how it had come to this. And how, barring some last-minute reprieve, this would be his last day. They had allowed him a visit earlier that morning from his wife, Jeannie, and his children, Marcus Jr. and Natishe. He had tried, unsuccessfully, to dissuade Jeannie from coming, because the visit had to take place behind the impersonal glass screens. The inability to touch and hold his wife and children one last time was nearly unbearable. Jeannie, of course, had cried and the children appeared bewildered. They were too young to fully understand what was going on and why Daddy had to leave them, but that he had no choice.

He glanced around. The silence of bare walls was broken by an open doorway leading to a bathroom and another door leading into the secured corridor. The room was furnished with a single bed—amazingly comfortable for and institutional facility—a small writing desk in case he wished to put any last thoughts on paper, a chair and a small table where he would eat his last meals. The only other furnishings were the television attached to the wall near the ceiling, the monitoring cameras, and an omnipresent digital clock mounted above the television. The general starkness of the room was in vivid contrast to his only direct connection with the outside world, and it was where his eyes finally came to rest.

On the wall opposite of where Marcus sat was an unbreakable glass window. Through it, he could see the red and purple remains of the Texas sunset silhouetting a high chain link fence and guarded gates. The scene evoked a strong memory of a similar but vastly different place. He was fifteen when he had been arrested and taken to juvenile detention. If he squinted he could almost feel he was once again in juvie. He recalled the choice that had sent him there—accepting a dare from his so-called "friends" to put on the Starter jacket and walking out of the store.

His thoughts tuned to his high school years and choices he'd made. He thought of the DARE program, when the two police officers had come to his central city school to warn and educate the students and the dangers of drugs and gangs. Ironically, it was only six weeks later that his brother Willie had been slain in a drive-by shooting. He thought of his mother, a hard-working but poorly educated domestic woman, who had wept uncontrollably for three days after the police chaplain had informed her of Willie's death. Marcus remembered how she had gotten on her knees and begged him to stay away from the drugs which had indirectly killed his brother. He thought of her plea to make something good of his life. He thought of his mother's sacrifice when she had sold her family home and moved to Kitsap County so he could escape their deteriorating neighborhood. His eyes teared as he realized he would never see his mother again. The doctors had given her less than a year to live. While he had talked to her by phone, her health had prevented her from making the journey from the West Coast for a final farewell.

Shaking his head, he brought his attention back to the present. A slight smile found its way to his otherwise stoic countenance. "It doesn't look like they will call the game on account of rain," he thought, remembering the old saying about *"red at night—a sailor's delight."*

This stray thought about game's being cancelled triggered memories of his favorite high school coach, who had pushed him to excel in sports. It had been Coach Biggers who had initially suggested the military might be his best chance to distance himself from the debilitating of his neighborhood. Had it only been a little over a year since he had been back to attend the Coach's memorial service? It seemed like a lifetime ago. He wondered what his coach would think of this latest and biggest game in which he was to be the featured player.

His hand reached for the remote and Marcus turned on the TV. He switched rapidly through the channels, pausing only briefly when he saw his picture displayed on the national news. Numerous requests for interviews had been passed on to his over the past three months. He had rejected all but two, using various excuses, but really because he felt they were primarily interested in trying to use his race and circumstances to further their own agendas.

He was not interested in being pseudopsychoanalyzed by various groups of self-serving commercial interests nor in being used to extol one race over another. This was not about race. After he was gone, they could do whatever they wanted.

Finally, he turned off the screen and lay back on the bed, hands clasped behind his head. Jumbled thoughts drifted in and out of his consciousness and sleep did not come easily. He knew a request for any medication would not be granted. His last conscious thought before drifting off into a fitful sleep was something his old coach, a master of cliches, had once said, *"The choices one makes early in life are the play diagrams of our future."*

Morning came. Marcus was awakened by the feel of a hand gently shaking his shoulder. He opened his eyes to see the figure of Dr. Emerson standing above him. Dr. Emerson was saying, "...need to conduct your final physical and prep."

Marcus groaned. He could see no need for another physical. For one thing, he was probably in better physical shape than ever in his life, with the possible exception during his years as an athlete. After all, what had he been doing the past few months except reading, eating and exercising—lots of exercising. Knowing however that the choice was not his, he stood and passively allowed the doctor to conduct his various tests, including tests for signs of drugs, even though how drugs could be obtained under the security measures employed here was incomprehensible.

The doctor concluded his examination and asked his patient how he was doing. Marcus surprised himself by admitting, "I'm nervous and I'm scared." He had always prided himself on not confiding his deepest emotional feelings to anyone except Jeannie, and reluctantly to the resident psychiatrist. But then, of course, he had never been in this situation before and it really didn't matter what he said. He thought to himself, *Maybe if I scream and yell, they will let me go home.* This offbeat thought was oddly comforting, maybe because while he knew he had no choice, the illusion provided some sense of balance.

The doctor and an assistant performed the other final necessary acts. His head was shaven, fingers and toenails trimmed, and his weight and height officially recorded. They left.

Once again, Marcus' thoughts turned to choices. This time he reflected on his decision regarding military service. He recalled talking to the Marine Corps recruiter. He had always considered himself "tough," so the Corps would be the initial choice should he decide to take that route. He thought, *I wonder what course my life would have taken had I chosen differently?* Certainly, he would not be where he was today.

The door opened again. He glanced at the clock. *It's too soon,* he thought, *they shouldn't be coming for me for another three hours.* He quickly realized that it was someone bringing his last meal. He looked at the food which he had ordered yesterday. His stomach turned. He wasn't sure he could eat. Nonetheless he motioned the server away and sat at the small table. After a few bites, he ate, attempting to savor every bite.

As he finished eating the door once again opened and Father Tidwell entered. The portly priest smiled and held out his hand. Marcus grasped the hand firmly and thanked him for coming. He had never been particularly religious, nor, in his mind, a very good Catholic. As a youth it had been easy to make excuses to himself about attending mass or confession. However, since coming here he felt he was beginning to make peace with God. He knew he was not there yet and questioned whether there was still time. He knew, regardless of the strength of his beliefs or the lack of them, he would be facing the ultimate challenge very shortly, and therefore, receiving the last rites wad necessary for him. Full acceptance of God, he now recognized as an important choice, one which perhaps he had put off for too long.

The absolutions completed, Marcus asked the priest if he would stay until they came. The large, athletic black man and the short, rotund priest sat talking about life and death, responsibility and choices. When the clock reached 12:00 he heard the military sounding steps echoing in the corridor. He rose, shook the priest's hand, and walked briskly to the door.

Two large uniformed men and two smaller men in civilian dress escorted him down the corridor and into an elevator. From the elevator they took a small underground shuttle to his destination. Arriving, they once again entered an elevator and rose to the cramped room with its single purpose equipment. He was helped into the requisite attire and seated into the form fitting chair. Technicians attached electrodes to his ankles, wrists and shaven head. A silvery helmet–like device was placed over his head and carefully seated into place.

The four men left after a few awkward words. He glanced around. Six other men remained in the room. It was with these technicians and a doctor that he would have to share any last thoughts. He wondered what they were thinking at this moment.

As final preparations were made he once again thought of choices, and of that last irrevocable choice which had brought him here. It had been made the evening of Coach Biggers funeral—when he had joined some of his former high school teammates at BBQ2U. They had toasted their former coach and shared memories, grief, and dreams. He had listened as they talked about their plans—plans dealing with easy money and low risks. It was there, somehow strangely appropriate, under the influence of past associations, a few drinks, and a darkened atmosphere that he had made his final decision.

Although he knew that his previous choices really had left him with no other choice that night.

He announced, seemingly to no one, "I am ready." He felt a shudder throughout his body as the powerful thrusters ignited. The shudder intensified and he was pushed back into his seat as the spacecraft lifted off.

At that moment, Colonel Marcus C. Washington, USMC Astronaut, knew that for him, regardless of the outcome, he had made the right choices. If successful, the seven year mission which he now commanded would be the first manned flight to Jupiter's moons and back.

DECEMBER

an empty place

Amber Rainey

I am a criminal.

I never thought I would utter those words. I have always been a good, upstanding citizen, trying to live my life while being a productive member of society. I have done my civic duty and voted in all the elections. I've written to my representatives to protest things I felt were unjust but still followed the laws as written until I could effect change in the world. I encouraged others to follow the proper channels and not be too rash. It almost pains me that I am now among those I once judged. I guess everyone has their breaking point and society has found mine. I still don't feel like I am above the law, although I am breaking it every single moment of every day. As it stands, I am a criminal, hiding from the authorities and constantly in fear of being discovered.

My alarm is going to go off in ten minutes. I don't really need it. I never do. The ultimate stress of preparing to leave for work each day has me silently going over my to-do list in my head. I don't really need the repetition because I could probably do it even if I were blind and deaf. I've been doing it for the last eleven years. Poppy knows I am awake.

She's started purring. It's her way of reassuring me and I have to admit that it is somewhat calming. We've got this routine down pat and she knows it. When the alarm does go off, she will stand up, give a good stretch (which I can hear in the quiet of the morning) and then wander off to sit in the sunlight coming through the mottled privacy window in the bathroom. She gets precious few moments in the light before I have to leave her for the day.

All this musing is especially poignant, given it is her birthday. Or, it is at least the day I have chosen for her birthday, as it is the closest approximation I could get of her age when I got her. Tonight, when I get home, I will give her a special tuna treat. It's one of her favorite things. I will sing *Happy Birthday* to her and we will celebrate another year together on this planet. My only hope is that she does not live long enough to witness me being dragged away by the authorities. She deserves a good life and I am trying to give her a safe one. I don't know if she understands any of it but she seems content with her life the way it is and she never gives me any trouble.

The alarm goes off and it startles me enough to make me jump. Poppy gives me an odd look and then proceeds to stretch, as I predicted. I turn off the alarm and give her an awkward scratch on the head. It is outside our usual routine and she seems indignant at the change. She gives me a little trilling sound, turns around, and hops off the bed to find her sunny spot. I sigh, wondering if the weight of my job or the stress of my situation is to blame then shrug to myself. It doesn't really matter what the cause of it is and I won't really be changing anything so I might as well just continue down my current path.

After a brief moment of allowing myself to lap in the luxury of self-pity, I throw back the blanket and get up from bed. I walk into the bathroom, where Poppy has claimed her spot and is content to let the warmth wash over her face.

My girl is getting old. She could probably stand to see a vet but that is impossible. Sometimes, I think she is starting to get a little senile. She doesn't seem to eat as much and occasionally she will look around as if she has lost me. If I quietly say her name, she looks up in recognition, gives a happy meow, and trots over to where I am sitting. It's almost as if she is saying, *Oh, there you are.* I can see the moment it clicks in her eyes—my poor kitty.

I'm finally done with my shower, dressing, and fixing my hair. I haven't worn makeup since I was a teenager and figured out that eschewing a painted face meant I could sleep longer. It takes me no time at all to get myself ready for work. It's all the rest of the morning chores that take up my time and the reason I have to get up so early. Once I am ready, I make sure that the cordoned-off section of my master closet has a clean litterbox, food, water, and a comfy bed prepared for Poppy for the day. It's hidden by a secret panel that is hidden behind my clothes. It isn't cramped but I would not exactly call it palatial. She doesn't seem to mind it too much. She knows exactly what to do and walks in there on her own. I give her some chin scratches.

"At least it's Friday. I'll be home soon and then we will have the whole weekend."

She slowly blinks at me with all the wisdom of an animal used to being given unnecessary explanations. I know it is more for me than it is for her but it is reassuring for me to tell her I have not abandoned her. One of my biggest fears is that I will be found out and she will waste away in a tiny closet away from the sunlight with not even her owner's body to eat. It's a morbid thought and I try to shake it off, even if I feel it deep in my bones. I give her one last pet and shut the concealment. She will be safe for another day. I often wonder how the time passes for her. I know she eats and sleeps. I would love to have a camera set up to watch her but I can't risk anyone hacking into it and ratting me out to the authorities.

Once Poppy is safely ensconced in her hiding spot, I set about cleaning my room and bathroom to make sure I get all of the cat hair she may have shed over the course of the previous evening and this morning. I vacuum off the comforter, then the floor, and then wipe down my counters in the bathroom. I vacuum the bathroom floor. Then I empty the contents of the vacuum in a small paper bag. I'll take the bag in my work satchel and then throw it in the furnace there to hide the evidence. I work in an animal aging center so I could be excused for having some pet hair around me but not as much as Poppy seems to produce.

Once I am satisfied with the cleanliness of my room, I open all of the curtains and blinds in my house. It's a formality really but if I don't follow this routine, my nosy neighbor will start asking questions and it will be the beginning of the end for me. I do one last check of my home and then take another deep breath. The next part of my difficult morning is about to begin.

"Oh, there you are," Mrs. Hanson waves and hurries to talk to me before I can get in my car. I mentally wince and then take a steadying breath and paste a smile on my face before turning to greet her.

"Hi, Mrs. Hanson."

"You are a little late today," she admonishes.

I check my watch. I know that I am exactly right on time but she makes every excuse to grill me every day. She has taken it upon herself to become a substitute mother to me ever since my own mother died and my wife left me. I don't really need her attention and would rather avoid it altogether but I can't afford to displease the neighborhood busybody. There are eyes everywhere and I am doing my best to avoid any kind of suspicion in order to keep Poppy safe. Alice once accused me of loving Poppy more than her and sometimes I am hard-pressed to remember how much I loved Alice. I had to let her go but she had to have some lingering feelings for me, at least, since she did not rat me out to the authorities. Not that I really thought she would, she is very anti-government. She and I were just different in that I did not believe in the lengths she was willing to go to and she thought I was wrong for working with the people who would see me incarcerated. Or worse. I digress though and she is waiting on my response.

"I'm a little tired. Work has been tough this week."

She nods. "You are doing God's work, honey. Do you know what you will do when the last ones are gone?"

She says the word *gone* as if these cats and dogs are going to take a vacation. They are all mostly older than Poppy and slowly, one by one, they are dying of old age and age-related diseases. We only have nine left. She is not wrong about me needing a new career path. I have no idea what I will be doing once I am not caring for geriatric animals. I try not to think about it because it reminds me I have one at home and the thought of losing her is upsetting. Once Poppy is gone, I will have nothing left of the people I love.

"No, ma'am. I try not to think about it. Just do my job well and hopefully there will be something for me at the end."

She pats my arm and I internally wince again. I am not a fan of being touched. "Well, dear, you'll find something. Did you remember to water those house plants?

I can go in and do it for you." She is always looking for an excuse to come into my house as if she knows I am hiding something and wants an opportunity to snoop around.

I nod. "Yes, ma'am, a happy plant is a happy home."

"Good. Good."

I can tell she is disappointed. However, she plasters on that sickeningly sweet expression she uses for me and starts to shuffle off. She stops, turns around, and gives me a searching stare. It almost gets uncomfortable but I'll be damned if I am going to let her crack my practiced calm. She nods to herself.

"Have a good day, dear."

"You, too!" I say cheerfully and get in my car.

I do my best not to look her away again but I can't help looking in the rearview mirror as I drive off. She has turned back towards where I was and is watching me. I watch her glance at the house and it turns my stomach. The last thing I need is for her to pry into my life. I have done everything I can to stay friendly with her and to keep her close but not too close. Something about her demeanor today gives me the willies.

I try to shake off the feeling but it preoccupies me during my drive to work. In what seems like no time at all I arrive at an aging building on the outskirts of town. It's tucked away behind the city's waste management transfer station. It's not a fluke for the building to be situated out of the public eye. Protesters used to picket out front but that was years ago.

Exactly twenty years ago, the end of legal pet ownership began. Humanity had survived a pandemic but during the time of lockdowns and forced home confinements, people adopted cats and dogs like crazy. Everyone wanted a reason to take a walk outside or break up the monotony of their days. Then, slowly, the world went back to the new normal. People returned to work. They went on with their lives. The animals that had brought them so much joy were now a burden and they began abandoning them in droves. Shelters couldn't keep up and even the ones who were no-kill had trouble maintaining their standards in the face of the overwhelming influx of unwanted pets.

The second pandemic hit, this time jumping from a house pet to a human. To this day, scientists cannot tell if it was from a cat or a dog but it didn't matter. Both species, and pet ownership in general, became the enemy. A convicted criminal and known pet hater had been elected as president. Someone who had his ear told him it was either eliminate the ability to own pets or shut the country down again. His conservative base was in an uproar over the possibility of lockdowns and mask mandates. He'd already become the dictator he had promised during his campaign so it made sense for him to just tell everyone they could no longer own pets. The law passed swiftly and the stacked, shady Supreme Court refused any involvement in ruling it illegal. The Constitution may as well have been shredded in that moment.

The law was simple. Every county in every state was required to build a "Center for Animal Welfare." The facility had to house every dog and cat from every household within the county. In larger urban areas, these facilities were massive complexes. Each county was also allowed to build a "Center for Aging Animals" to house the elderly pets. The ones that tended to need more care and more nurturing at the end stages of their lives. It could have been worse. Any pets not of the feline or canine species were either let out into nature or euthanized. Stores were no longer allowed to sell animals of any kind to human owners. Livestock were exempt from this policy but no one gets a horse as an apartment pet. Pets of any kind were now illegal.

The new pet centers ran on a mix of paid staff and volunteers. It was a pet lover's dream to volunteer and applications were required. Background checks were mandatory and people signed waivers to allow random searches of their person and their vehicles. It was a highly sought-after position. In the early days, I passed many picket lines of protesters of the laws, as well as witnessed many volunteers carted off to jail for trying to clandestinely take an animal. In the beginning, each incident would shake me to my core. Eventually, I learned to hide my inner turmoil and mask my emotions. I was always worried about Poppy.

I had been working at the Center for Animal Welfare for a year. I enjoyed my job because I felt lucky to be able to interact with the cats. I had always loved cats but did not have any when the law banning pet ownership was passed. My beloved Luna had just passed away from cancer and I had not been ready to get another cat. Perhaps I would have felt differently about the law if I'd still owned one of my own. Alice thinks I would have fought harder against it. She always seemed so disappointed in me for taking a job with the people she loathed.

The day started as normal as any other day. I went to work and made sure all the cats were fed and watered. A coworker and I changed the litter and mopped the floors. I did some laundry and had just settled into a community cat room to give the residents some attention when the alarm sirens began. I followed protocol, sanitizing my hands on the way out of the room and exiting the building to meet at my designated gathering point. There were whispers but no one seemed to know what was happening. It was incredibly humid that day. We'd been having a lot of unseasonal thunderstorms and the skies looked ready to burst at any moment. After what seemed like an eternity, our manager came out of the building with a sour expression.

"We've had a breach and security has decided to shut us down for the day. Your cars have been searched and if I call your name, please proceed into the building. The rest of you will then be able to gather your things and leave."

Murmurs arose throughout our ranks. We waited patiently and our manager called out the names of three people. I made eye contact with a coworker and she looked as puzzled as I was. None of the three people they were seeking was among our group. I shrugged and mouthed the words I have no idea. After a few more moments, my manager spoke quietly with the head of security. He nodded and walked off.

"Y'all are dismissed. Gather your things as quickly as possible and leave the premises. I expect you back on Monday morning unless you are given other instructions over the weekend."

It did not take any time at all for everyone to begin moving. I found my friend and we started to follow the rest of our coworkers inside. When we neared our manager, he put his arm out to stop us. I gave a startled expression to my coworker and she looked just as concerned.

"Katherine, I need a word," he said.

I nodded and then stepped to the side. My coworker raised her eyebrows and I shrugged again. She nodded back at me and then went inside after glancing back for a split second. I waited next to my manager while the rest of my coworkers filtered inside. The heat, coupled with the stares from the stragglers, was making me feel light-headed. My manager spent the time doing something on his phone that seemed to displease him even further. Everyone was finally inside when my manager turned his attention to me.

"Have you noticed anything strange in the cat rooms?"

I was genuinely perplexed by the question. "No, sir. What do you mean?"

"Any new volunteers that seem to be too friendly with the staff? Anything fishy?" he pushed.

"No. Nothing. It's been rather quiet. Mitzi has been… "

"I'm not talking about the individual cats, nor do I care about their personalities. I'm asking you about the people." He was getting angry at me and I winced. This was before I was good at hiding it. This seemed to soften his demeanor. "I apologize. You're dismissed. See you Monday."

He turned and opened the door, waiting for me to go inside. I tried to put as much space between us as I entered and then hurried to my locker to grab my things. It was like a ghost town already, with everyone having already been escorted out. A security guard was waiting for me outside the locker room and silently stepped in front of me to lead me to the parking lot. I was slightly perturbed by the escort but did not say anything on the subject. The atmosphere was clearly tense and we would probably never know the extent of what was happening. Management liked to sweep these incidents under the rug and pretend they did not happen although it was less rare than you can imagine.

When I got to my car, I fumbled for the keys and the security guard grew visibly impatient. I could tell he did not enjoy his job and was ready to be done with me. I tried to put on an apologetic but reassuring smile.

"I've got it. I just need to empty this on my hood and I'm sure my keys are in here. I'll be out of here in a jiff!" I said cheerily.

He squinted his eyes at me and then nodded. "Make sure you are gone within the next few minutes."

I nodded and he seemed satisfied. He walked off shaking his head and mumbling under his breath. I let out a breath I did not know that I was holding. He'd been intimidating and it was beyond my ability to function, let alone find my keys, under such a withering stare. It was easy to find them once I was alone and I walked over to my door to open it. To my surprise, it was already unlocked. I am a creature of habit and I was pretty sure it had been locked that morning but I shrugged it off, got in my car, and drove home. I pulled into the garage. We'd been parking my car in the garage during this time to keep it out of the weather. Nowadays, I don't park in the garage because I fear forgetting to put the door down and Mrs. Hanson finding a reason to enter my house. Alice wouldn't be home for a few more hours so I would have the place all to myself. I was just getting out of the car when I heard a small noise coming from the backseat.

My initial glance into the backseat and floorboard ended in confusion as I did not see anything. I almost shrugged off hearing anything when I heard it again—a distinct mewling sound. I looked around quickly, feeling anxious about what I was about to find and then glanced out the back window of my car at the open garage door. I quickly shut the door and got out of the driver's seat. Taking a deep breath, I pulled open the back passenger door, then looked under the front seat. There was a tiny towel under there and it was moving and mewling. My heart began racing. I grabbed the towel, glancing around again and attempting to reassure myself I was alone in the garage. My thoughts were a jumbled mess. I ran inside our house and into my bathroom, shutting the doors behind me. It was the only room in the house without windows thrown open to the world.

I set the tiny bundle on my counter and began to open it. Gasping, I found a tiny kitten, possibly four weeks old squirming around and mewling in hunger. She was a little brown tabby with orange spots and was the most adorable, fluffy thing I had seen in years. All of the surrendered pets were now past the kitten stage and well into adulthood. Where on earth had this kitten come from and who had put it in my car? I almost could not comprehend what I was seeing but my brain went into action mode and my emotions shut off for the moment. The baby needed food and warmth.

I had to make do with what he had on hand but I was able to cook up a little chicken and add some broth to it. The kitten scarfed it down as if she had never eaten a day in her life. Once she was fed, I placed her in a shoebox with a neck warming pad in my closet. I hadn't realized how much time had passed but I heard Alice coming in through the door. I quickly shut my closet and straightened the bathroom before rushing out to greet her.

"Hi!" I said too loudly and awkwardly. She was immediately suspicious.

"What have you done?"

I laughed nervously, "I don't know what you mean."

"What. Have. You. Done?" she persisted.

I swallowed the lump in my throat. I didn't know how this conversation would end. Alice loved animals. She had spent years protesting the bans and picketing in front of the welfare center. We'd had arguments over my job. She wouldn't turn me in. I just didn't know what to do and what she would suggest. I hadn't had time to think yet and she was too good at reading me. We would do whatever she decided and I was not yet sure if it was a good or bad thing.

"It's in the closet," I said and turned around. I knew she was following me and I could hear her exasperated sigh loud and clear. I stopped for a moment outside the door and she began tapping her foot.

"Now, Kat."

I nodded, swallowing hard and opening the closet door. I breathed an internal sigh of relief that the kitten was still asleep in the shoebox. I stepped into the closet and out of the way, bending down to the shoe box. It took her a moment to see what I was looking at and then she dropped to her knees, for once at a loss for words. She looked at the kitten and then back at me, her mouth hanging open.

When she was finally able to speak, her voice trembled. "Where did you get it?"

I shrugged. "It was in my car."

"What do you mean? Kittens don't just appear in cars. This shouldn't even be possible. They altered all of them."

"Well, apparently not all of them. She's real," I said as I gestured to the kitten in the box.

"It's a she?" She stroked the tiny kitten's head and it started to purr. A tear started down Alice's cheek.

"What do we do? I don't know where she came from. We had an incident at the center today and they sent everyone home. My manager was asking odd questions and then I get home and there is a kitten shoved under the driver's seat. I don't know how she got there or who put her there or why they chose me. We have to turn her in..."

"No!"

I jumped back at the force in her voice as she cut me off. She scooped up the tiny kitten and cradled it against her chest. Several more tears ran down her cheeks and I felt guilty for even suggesting it. Alice was outwardly very butch and strong but she was a softy at heart. She felt things more deeply than anyone I knew and I could see she was already in love with the creature in her hand. She gave me an apologetic smile and reached a hand out to grab mine. I put my other hand on top of hers and stroked it to reassure her.

"I'm sorry. We can't turn it in. You'll lose your job."

"You never liked me working there anyway."

She nodded. "True. However, now we are going to need stuff you can only get from there."

I shook my head in horror. She was implying that I should steal things from my job for this little cat. It was dangerous. We could go to jail just for owning the cat but stealing things and owning a cat was a recipe for all kinds of repercussions from the government. We would never work again if we were caught and that would mean losing everything. I instinctively knew she would want to keep the cat but I did not know the lengths she would want me to go to for it.

"Kat, it will need food."

"I can cook for it."

"What about vaccines?"

"How am I supposed to steal vaccines? Why does she need them. It's not like she would ever see the light of day to be exposed to anything."

"Sweetheart," she put on her coaxing voice, the one she knew I could not resist, "maybe not now, but she might need something and your job might protect her. No one will suspect we have her. You have been a model employee."

"I haven't been a criminal."

I could see the jolt of hurt in her eyes at my statement. I hadn't meant it to come out the way it did but relistening to it in my head made me realize I'd hit out at her. I didn't want to pain her and I didn't want to rehash old arguments. It was water under the bridge and we both knew it.

"I'm sorry. That was rude." I sighed and looked at my wife holding the tiny proof that I was already on my way to being a criminal because I hadn't turned her in the moment I found her. I closed my eyes and took a deep breath. When I opened them, I nodded in resignation. She let out a little snort of glee that was uncommon to her and I giggled. She smiled so big I felt like my heart would burst.

"What are we going to name her?"

Alice looked up from the kitten and grinned. "How about Poppy? She's beautiful and like a drug with her little toe beans and purrs."

I nodded. "I like that."

Poppy seemed to like it too as she looked up at me and meowed, then snuggled back against Alice. I smiled at the two of them and wished I could take a picture. Then I silently reprimanded myself. A picture would be very damning evidence if it ever got into the wrong hands. I looked around my closet and began making a mental checklist of everything that would need to happen in order to keep Poppy, and us, safe. We had a lot of work to do.

Someone knocked on my car window and my head almost hit the roof of the car when I jumped. I'd been so lost in my memories I had not noticed my boss standing outside my car. I gave a little wave, turned off the car and opened the door. He stepped aside while I exited and waited for me to explain.

"I guess I was daydreaming," I said sheepishly.

"Mmm. You know security does not like it when we dawdle."

"Yes, sir." He did not say anything else and I followed behind him into the building.

I'd transferred to the Center for Aging Animals just after Alice left. Every subversive act she did against the centers made me fear not only for her but also for Poppy. It became an obsession. It's not that I did not love Alice but I felt like she was putting everyone else above her own family and it caused a lot of tension. She finally decided that our goals were no longer compatible and she accused me of caring more about being a *good girl* than being a decent human. I'd laughed at that, telling her that good girls were not criminals. She'd turned without a word and left the house. When I came home from work the next day, there was a note and all her things were gone. She'd left Poppy with me. I guess she knew I would still take care of our cat, even if I could not agree with her on how it should be done.

In the beginning, the center was jam-packed with older cats and dogs. Eventually, the main welfare centers shut down as all the animals in their care were either dead or seniors. Very few aging centers even had dogs anymore. Dogs rarely live as long as cats and so the centers for aging animals have all been mostly adapted for cats only. It is a decent home for the cats. Some centers only have small kennels but I was able to convince the designers of our center to give the cats big community rooms and giant kennel rooms for the cats needing more specialized care. It was a nice retirement home and the best I could do for these amazing creatures.

I set about doing my daily tasks and getting lost in the comforting sameness of it all. I checked on some of the older cats and did my best to give each of them more attention than normal. George would not be with us much longer but he was a trooper and was hanging on, despite his advanced age. He'd come in already nearing his senior years and he had to be close to twenty years old. He had to eat special food and was unable to be in a community room. He was a huge, beautiful orange tabby with a loud purr and the desire to be held like a baby. He liked me to sing while holding him and petting his head. He would always close his eyes in bliss. I was just returning him to his kennel when the alarms began blaring. It was odd as I had not heard that sound in years. No one really bothered with the senior animals.

I closed George's kennel door and went outside to my meeting point. We only had five staff members at our center. The rest were volunteers and today we only had two. As I joined the others, Andrew came up to me.

"Know what this is about?" he asked. He was young and had probably never been through one of these security protocol alarms.

"No."

My boss came outside with the head of security. He searched the crowd and then gave a slight nod when his eyes met mine. I tried to hide the concern in my eyes but I am not sure if I was successful. I had felt uneasy all day like some impending sense of doom was coming. I was unsettled and it was beginning to crack my perfectly crafted facade. Something big was happening and I did not like the storm that was brewing.

"Katherine, I need to speak with you after this." As I nodded, he spoke to the rest of those gathered with me. "We've had an incident and need to shut down for the day. All of the cats have been fed, therefore you are dismissed. You will be paid for a full day. Thank you."

The sense of déjà vu was uncanny. This boss was always nicer, if more terse, than my former boss, but the words were just so similar. I'd been reminiscing all day and it felt as if the universe was reading my mind and making me relive the major points. It was not a welcome experience.

I waited until everyone went inside and then followed my boss into the building and into his office. "Have a seat."

I sat, looking around at the walls. He had his animal care certifications and some pictures of animals we'd lost over the years. I was fairly certain he was an animal lover but I knew he had the hardest job of any of us. He was responsible for the euthanasia of the cats no longer able to live a good life. I am certain he had to disassociate from the residents in order to have some peace of mind. He'd never been very sociable although he did talk to us kindly when necessary and ordered us lunch on occasion. I was broken out of my musings by him clearing his throat.

"Do you know Alice Kang?"

My head almost jolted back at the question and my heart jumped to my throat. I nodded because I could not speak.

"She is your wife?"

I shook my head, stopped, then nodded. We'd never gotten a divorce. I'd actually never taken off my wedding ring. I looked down at it and it suddenly felt odd on my finger. "I haven't seen her in five years."

"Why not?" he asked, not obtrusively but it was a private question.

I shrugged. "We had different ideal lives and she did not like my vision for our future."

"Are you aware she just got out of prison?"

My head snapped up and I stared him down. He was telling the truth. His face did not waver. He leaned slightly forward and that broke the momentary tension. "I didn't... no."

"Katherine, someone attempted to break in today. The same day your wife gets out of prison for breaking into another facility and you mean to tell me you know nothing of this development?"

"No, sir. I don't know why I was never contacted about her being in prison. Why didn't they question me when it first happened?"

He leaned back in his chair, considering. Then he pulled out a thick folder and opened it, leafing through the pages before stopping somewhere near the middle.

"They had you under surveillance and you are squeaky clean. They determined that you were not a party to her actions. Mrs. Hanson, your neighbor, testified on your behalf and cleared your name. Apparently, your wife asked them to keep you out of it."

Tears sprang to my eyes. I didn't know what she had been through and I would have been there for her if she'd only let me know. She'd protected Poppy as much as she had protected me. I was surprised to learn of Mrs. Hanson's involvement.

"If Alice contacts you, you will let me know so I can alert the proper authorities?"

I thought a moment. He was asking me to rat out the woman I still loved. I was already a criminal. I could add lying to the list and not be any worse for it. I nodded.

He studied me for another moment and seemed to find reassurance in what he saw. "Good. I'll see you on Monday."

I was clearly being dismissed so I got up and left his office. We no longer had security follow us around so I took my time checking that the cats were all settled for the night, saying goodnight to each one. I gathered my things and went to my car. I resisted the urge to rest my head on the steering wheel. I did not want to look any more suspicious than I felt.

I drove home in an almost zombie-like state. I don't even remember pulling into the driveway. I shut off the car and looked around. Sighing heavily, I spotted Mrs. Hanson watering her flowerbeds. I'd have to deal with her again and it was almost too much but if I rushed inside it would arouse suspicion. I gathered my thoughts and my satchel, realizing too late that Poppy's bag of hair was still inside of it. I hadn't gotten to eat lunch and therefore hadn't been to the incinerator. I made sure the satchel was zipped up tight before hefting it onto my shoulder and stepping out of the car.

I waved at Mrs. Hanson and waited for her to shut off the water. She smiled and waved back at me. "You're home early today. Are you sick?"

I tried not to grit my teeth. Maybe there was concern in her voice but she was always prying. She'd been supportive when Alice left but it had also felt like she was judging. She'd say things about my wife that felt like sniping and it was always grating to me. She was a prickly, nosy old woman and I resented her busybody ways.

"No, ma'am. There was a security incident and they sent us home for our safety. I am sure it's nothing."

"I see. Well, you had a package delivery earlier. I'll just go inside and grab it. I did not want it sitting on your porch forever and your spare key is still missing. You need to replace that!"

I rolled my eyes at her back as she retreated to retrieve my package. My spare key had been *missing* for a very long time precisely to keep her out of my house. Truthfully, it was just hidden in a different place. I did not like that she took my packages inside her house but I never got anything that would get me in trouble so it was just inconvenient and not dangerous. She came outside with a large envelope, which was odd because those were normally delivered in our cluster boxes.

"They wanted a signature for it so I signed for you, dear."

I took the package from her, "Thank you, Mrs.

Hanson. I haven't had lunch yet so I am going to go inside now."

"Okay, dear."

She watched me like a hawk as I went inside. I leaned back against the front door and then put the envelope on the counter. I took my time making lunch and settling in at the counter. I looked over at the kitchen table. I never ate there anymore, it always felt too big. Alice and I used to have parties and cookouts but that all stopped when Poppy came into our lives. I once read a home without pets was an empty place and it would never be more true in my life once Poppy was gone. She was the sole reason I had any sanity left. I briefly toyed with the idea of going to let her out of her hiding place but that would mean closing the curtains early and Mrs. Hanson was still doing her yardwork. Any change in my routine and she would take it as a sign to pry further.

I took a bit of my lunch and then picked up the package. It didn't feel too heavy but had an odd-shaped lump in it. I tore open the top and pulled out a notecard. I turned it upside down and a key fell out of the envelope. The notecard was in a plain white envelope without anything written on it. I picked up the key and it looked just like a house key. I pulled out the notecard. An address was written on it in a very familiar handwriting. My hands began shaking. I quickly pulled up a map on my phone and started to put in the address, then took a moment. If this was her, they might be watching me or tapping my phone. I quickly ate my lunch and then threw the notecard and key into my satchel. I grabbed the bag of fur out of the satchel and hid it under the frozen pizza in my freezer. It was the best I could do on such short notice.

I found an out-of-the-way internet cafe and went to

a computer in the back. I'd paid for an incognito VPN so I logged in and searched the address on the notecard. My pulse was skyrocketing and I tried to do some calming breaths. The address was for a storage unit on the edge of town. I guess the key was for the "apartment number" written on the notecard. It was a twenty-four-hour building. I glanced at the clock. Mrs. Hanson would notice if I did not come back home on time. For once, I cursed myself for being such a creature of habit. I would have to go home and go back out later, once she had gone to bed.

After I returned home, it was finally a decent time to shut all the windows and have a kitty birthday party. Poppy meowed at me cheerfully and stretched her long body out of her hiding place. She rubbed up against my legs and I picked her up, burying my face in her fur. She always had a calming effect on me. I prepared her tuna and sang to her. I don't know if she appreciated the singing as much as George does but she happily ate her tuna and then set about grooming herself while I made myself dinner. I was not really hungry but I needed something to occupy the time because the later it got, the more antsy I felt. The impending doom was back, stronger than ever.

I was startled for what felt like the millionth time today by the doorbell and my home assistant announcing, *"Someone is at the front door."* I momentarily looked at Poppy in a panic. She seemed to understand and took herself into the bedroom. I quickly picked up the empty bowl from the floor and put it in the sink. I composed myself and went to the front door. When I opened it, Mrs. Hanson was standing there.

"Hello, dear. I made this cake and wanted to share some with you." She said as she handed me a foil wrapped plate.

"Umm, thank you." She'd never really shared any baked goods with me before. It was definitely out of the ordinary.

"No worries. Be sure to eat it tonight as it won't be good tomorrow. See you later, dear."

She turned and left so quickly that I wondered if it was the same woman I had lived next to all these years. I hadn't had to get out of the conversation with her. My day just kept getting more and more weird. I set the cake down on the counter and lifted the foil. A piece of chocolate cake was under the foil but there was another notecard taped to the bottom of the foil. Poppy peeked around the corner and meowed at me and I shrugged at her as if she would understand that I had no idea what was happening anymore than she did. I opened the notecard.

Go to bed as usual. They are watching you. At 1 am, come out the back door and climb through the broken slat. My back door will be open. Get in the back floorboard of my car and stay hidden. Do not speak. Bring the key. Mrs. H.

I reread the note close to twenty times. I had so many questions. Who was watching me? What did Mrs, Hanson know about Alice? How was Mrs. Hanson capable of such subterfuge? I'd always thought she was the first person who would turn in a criminal. Maybe I had misjudged her. My head was spinning. I sat heavily on my couch and Poppy jumped into my lap and started purring. I knew she could tell something was off and she was doing her best to comfort me. The clock chimed ten and I jumped into action. I had to make it appear that I was doing all my normal things. I got ready for bed, turned out the lights, and lay down, knowing I would not get any rest.

It was fifteen minutes to 1 am. I quietly woke Poppy and picked her up, explaining that she would need to hide until I returned home. She seemed understanding, if not annoyed and got into her bed. I concealed her spot and then grabbed a black jacket, both for warmth and stealth. I quietly opened the back door and crept across the yard to the rear of my fence where it abutted Mrs. Hanson's yard. Sure enough, the broken slat moved easily, as if it had been prepared for me to pass through. I took a moment in her yard, briefly wondering if I was being set up and then thought better of letting that idea take root. I went into her back door, through her living room, and down the hall to the garage door. None of her lights were on and there were no signs of movement. I opened the garage and got into the car as instructed.

I don't know how long I waited but I finally heard her come into the garage and then she was in the drivers seat. We started along and I wished I could see where we were going. The thought of being handed over to the authorities crossed my mind again and I did my best to block it out. I tried to recognize the trees and signs flashing over my head but there was no way to actually know where I was based on that information. I was thankful the floorboard was a decent size and flat, instead of the kind that had a hump in the middle. Finally, we stopped.

"We are here, dear."

I hesitated and then sat up. We were in front of a storage building. It was the one from the first notecard. I blinked a few times and then gave her a questioning look with a raised eyebrow.

"She's waiting for you," she said as she motioned towards the building.

I got out of the car and entered the building. I looked at the directions to the unit for which I had a key and then quickly found it. I opened the door with the key and stepped into the unit. Alice and two other people were sitting inside.

"Hey, Kat. How've you been?" she said it as if we'd just seen each other.

I couldn't say anything and was frozen to my spot. Mrs. Hanson came in behind me and closed the door. She looked between me and Alice and then nodded, coming to a decision. She walked over to a chair and motioned to it.

"Perhaps you would like to sit down, dear?"

I looked at her and nodded, making my way to the chair and slowly sitting down. Alice came over and kneeled in front of me, softly caressing my hands in reassurance the way I used to do for her. The other two people went to the back of the unit and sat down, quietly conversing with each other. Mrs. Hanson stood behind Alice and looked at me with sympathy in her eyes. I shook my head, trying to think of something to say and failing to form any coherent thoughts. After waiting for Alice to say something and getting nothing from her, I looked up at Mrs. Hanson.

"Yes, dear. This is very shocking. I am sure it is good to see Alice. She's been so worried about you. Especially since the incident at the center today."

My eyes glanced at Alice, who was shaking her head. "Was it you?" I croaked.

"No. But I know who it was. I told them not to do it at that center but they wouldn't listen."

"What did they do?" I had no idea what caused a security incident. I knew none of the cats were harmed or taken but not what shut us down for the day.

She sighed. "They stole some vaccines. Our agent was stupid and left the cabinet open. As she exited the room, a security guard was passing her in the hallway and he caught sight of it. She was acting as a new volunteer so she'd already had a random search the day before and thought she could get away with it. She was too cocky and out to prove to us she was useful."

"Us?"

"The Organization, dear."

I looked at Mrs. Hanson as if she'd grown an extra head. It was very new to me that she would be in on all this intrigue and I don't think it had fully registered. It all felt like a dream. I reached down and pinched my arm and both she and Alice chuckled. The others behind me stopped talking for a moment and Alice gave a slight nod. They went back to their conversation.

"You are awake. This can all be daunting at first but you will get used to it." She stood and then pulled up a chair next to mine. Mrs. Hanson did the same thing. "Mamie, would you like to explain? You do it better than me."

Mrs. Hanson nodded and turned to me. "You see, dear, we are an organization for the prevention of the extinction of dogs and cats. We have been operating since the beginning of the ban on pet ownership. I recruited Alice after she was arrested and sentenced so many years ago. We have a facility out in the country and we place animals with good homes. We are working on getting the laws changed again and when that happens we will be able to open adoption centers to the public."

"We are close to the law changes, Kat. Imagine allowing Poppy to roam the house freely in her golden years. Maybe even getting her a little brother or sister to teach the ropes to for when she is gone."

I gave Alice a look and Mrs. Hanson chuckled again.

"I've known about your sweet girl from the beginning. Mine's name is Zorro. It used to be one of my favorite shows as a child."

My head swung so fast I almost gave myself whiplash. "You have a cat?"

She smiled broadly, "Why yes, he is a beautiful Russian Blue. It's a bear dealing with his fur but he does love his brushies. The fur makes wonderful natural nesting material for the birds in our yards."

I could see the pride she took in both owning the cat and providing for the wild animals in our neighborhood. I'd always wondered why the bird's nest in her tree looked fluffy. Now I knew where it was coming from. I had to admit my opinion of Mrs. Hanson was drastically changing. I'd never have pegged her as a cat lover.

"Of course, I would love to have a dog but we cannot safely have them, especially with them watching your house so closely. Alice was a little too zealous in her activities."

Alice looked down sheepishly and I could see her cheeks redden. She never got embarrassed easily and I could imagine her getting a scolding from the older woman. Mrs. Hanson patted her knee and then turned back to me.

"We'd like to bring you on board. You have a lot of knowledge from all your time at the center."

"I don't know if I could abandon them. I've been caring for them for so long. I just couldn't..." I was trying not to choke up.

"Sweetheart, I wouldn't ask you to leave them. You could just come to help us on the weekends at the new facility. The volunteer who caused the problems at your center is going to turn herself in. They will clear my name. I'd like to come home if you will let me." She was pleading with me. It was another new experience. She was giving me an actual choice.

"I will give you two a moment, dear." Mrs. Hanson

stood up and went over to the other two people. She spoke with them and then they too stood. The three of them left the room. Alice and I sat in the quiet while I thought over everything that was happening. I didn't know what to do. I still didn't understand the depth of what they wanted from me. Hiding Poppy had always been illegal but now I felt like a whole new level of criminal activity was being presented to me and I did not know how to feel about it.

Alice broke the silence. "Do you remember when we first got engaged and we were lying in the grass at the park and I asked you what your greatest fear was?"

I nodded. It had been a totally wonderful day and one of my happiest memories. I was so in love with her. I was still in love with her. It was as if the last five years had been only a few hours. I wanted her to enfold me in her arms and never let go. I was certain we would get to that point but we had a lot to hash out before it happened. Nevertheless, my arms itched at the thought of being in her embrace. I smiled.

"Your greatest fear was never having chocolate again." I laughed.

She grinned. "It was kind of a petty fear. Yours was much deeper but you've always had such complex ideas in that genius brain of yours."

I shrugged, always embarrassed when she complimented me. "My greatest fear was letting you down."

"I told you that would never happen."

I shook my head. "But I did and you left."

A tear coursed down her cheek. I reached up to wipe it away and she caught my hand. She kissed my fingers and I shivered at the feeling. She smiled sadly. "I am the one who let you down. I thought I was doing something for you but it was really about me. Then I got caught being rash and paid for it."

"They told me you went to prison. Why didn't you tell me? Maybe I could have helped."

"No," she sighed. "It would not have helped anything. It's not your fault and we can talk about it, or argue about it, or ignore it at some later date. I know this has been overwhelming tonight."

I nodded. "True. The most shocking of all is knowing that Mrs. Hanson is a criminal mastermind."

Alice chuckled again. "That woman is very surprising. She's done a great job of looking out for you."

"Yes, she has annoyed the shit out of me every day since you left. She never skips a day!" I protested.

"Good. It's helped me know you were safe."

I rolled my eyes at her. I knew I was still processing the whirlwind of information. It would take some time to get a handle on all of it. I was certain of two things. I wanted Alice back and I wanted to help her cause. It was enough.

"Do you know what my greatest fear is now?" I asked. She shook her head. "A world without pets."

"Well, I think you can help us keep that from happening. It won't be legal, though"

"I'm not sure I care anymore. Come home and we can talk about it. Poppy will be mad if you don't wish her a belated Happy Birthday. You'd better have tuna!" I stood up and held out my hand.

She grinned widely as she stood and shocked me by embracing me in the strongest bear hug she had ever given me. After a moment, I relaxed into her and rested my head against her shoulder. She relaxed too and hugged me less tightly but did not let go as she rested her head on top of mine. Suddenly, the impending sense of doom turned into one of hope. The day had begun with memories and was ending with new beginnings.

I am a criminal. My neighbor and my wife are criminals. There are more of us than anyone could imagine and we are slowly growing in numbers. We don't want to be criminals but our society is forcing our hand and until we can make our activities legal, we will continue working behind the scenes to make things right. Perhaps our greatest fear should not be about being criminals but in not fighting for what is right.

I'm not alone. That is what matters the most.

THIRTEEN

backmasking

Pauline Uglade

Our point of view smash cuts from a man's— woman's?—middle finger stabbing through the air toward the camera, to a whirling chainsaw. It hurtles down a hallway in hot pursuit of a man. Flurries of reaction shots whiplash between it and his face. He can't outrun the chainsaw, as his shoes that cost more than a month's pay skid on the stairs. The motor revs on its own, the stylized, peaking waveform almost deafening his screams as the chainsaw windmills off the second floor balcony and plummets past the railing. The drugs coursing through him, snorted during debauched parties, where he flaunted his extravagant wealth with gaudy goods, sabotage him.

His torso falls into the glimmering chain. A split screen of his dismembered legs splatting against one wall of the lobby, and his body from the groin up, thudding to the ground feet away from the lobby's entrance, expands to fill the frame. Our view fades to black.

The chainsaw returns to me, my memories, where it belongs. It's not a CGI animation, or a functional, but dulled deathtrap. The man's mortal fear compelled his death into existence: He believed in me, so he became my victim.

The man—or woman—they could be an alien who labored for millennia to reach me. They could be an AI with embodied intelligence who lacked emotional nuance. Their actions matter, not who they are.

They scrabble backward, fumbling for a wallet in a breast pocket. I'd only see a shirt approximating theirs on TV, a life cast, or a corpse. Hell—my friends and I could buy ten outfits with the fabric alone.

"Please—I'll do anything!"

A wad of cash throws itself to the floor, pleading for clemency. My rage saturates the object, impatient enough to preempt postproduction and hindsight. Of course, they can't see the red filter taped over my vision. To them, a greenscreen and a screensaver are one in the same. I've spent more time hauling a camera than they have counting their metaphorical money.

I pocket the compensation, enough to fill a tank of gas. "So now you surrender your profits? When you're this close to getting your head put on a stick—"

I tighten my fist around an ax leveled at their face, but no drugs or alcohol cloud their judgment. I'm not staging their kidnaping like a dance. I don't extol the virtues of what I love, and how they'll never appreciate my favorite works of art and pop culture. "You didn't help when I isolated myself at home for the greater good."

An email flashes onscreen. It encroaches on shots of my unkempt bedroom, a physical filter bleaching it white and stripping it of personality like an office cubicle. The camera zooms in, until it pinpoints my prone body, reading the email in bed. The camera fixes on a sentence in the body text, buzzwords piercing my custom browser and computer: *We are committed to every employee's success in these difficult times. NO MATTER how long they've worked here.*

I inject my evidence, my dread, into them, my contempt flecking onto their face with every word. "Can you imagine what it felt like? For Dr. Fauci to sit me down at the TV and tell you that if I went outside, I'd die?"

Freeze frames depict me hurling a fistful of cash onto a gas station counter, in exchange for lottery tickets. I present my ID for formality's sake. Each freeze frame invades their vision and blankets the office walls. The cashier and the nearest employee gape, visible even behind their masks, but don't comment. Instead, they nod at each other.

"I didn't write that—I didn't intend—"

My retort cleaves their face open. Not their skull, but the façade. "You didn't care when I was a month's rent from eviction."

This time, freeze frames of a stark white apartment accompany me, a mental air drop. Vintage eighties furniture, appliances, and art, intercut with items created or purchased with love. Most even bare signatures from friends I've known long enough that my family welcomed them in, even before they met those friends in person. In split screen, I juxtapose these closeups with a montage of my remotely arranged, outdoor, masked sales of each item. Raw, mumble core audio accentuates my concurrent sobs.

My tears don't denature my venom. "To hell with good intensions!"

They bang on the wall with their elbow. The desperation, the desire to be heard, overwhelms the imminent threat of the ax blade, parallel to their mouth. I automate the mixing process with a blunt, spoken prompt. "Remove all silence from this track."

Their mouth works, as their noise ceases. Replacing their audio, a voice clone parrots my deafening shouts of pain. The voice clone completes my prompt, with neither delays nor complaints, like what my employers want, rather than pay me more, or credit me for my work. The silence and voice acting reach them, even though they've never touched a digital audio workstation before.

I lean in. My warnings of hallucinated suffering surround us. My rebuttal tips the needle, revolving and scraping between their ears. "Your generation smothered my future. Because you thought everything was better, four years ago."

The ensuing reply highlights their lie. "I didn't! I didn't vote for—"

Without moving, I zip-tied them to the makeup chair and compelled them to discard every aspect of their character. Color drains from their face. Their confidence dissolves and assertive posture sluffs off. The unraveling threads in their wardrobe, the makeup smothering their skin, expose their costume.

The reversion completes. Voices echoing from offscreen provide the score. The reverb of empty lots and debris strewn hallways penetrate the soundproofing that my will holds aloft. "Where is he?"

They perk up, relief repressing their fear over their lack of control. I imagine they think, *This nightmare is over. I can leave. I've driven this depraved psychopath out of here! My colleagues and I can proceed, like a normal morning.*

"Did Errin make it?"

The crashing of upended furniture, the bang of closet and soundstage doors, jars our bones. Shaky cam points of view project on the walls, not in their mind's eye. Their pupils dilate, at the bullet holes crafted on office workstations and through makeshift barricades. Panicked, but clear ADR skewers the din encompassing us.

"What do they want?"

"Why take Errin as a hostage?"

The board member gapes, even as I arc the ax toward them. "That's not true—"

I press the ax handle onto their forehead. I import the finished product into their mind: The police's crime scene recreation, augmented with voice overs of forged manifestos, with meaningless confessions. In it, they grip the ax instead, and I'm flush against the wall. Torrents of sweat and tears erase four hours of makeup and prosthetics, applied before dawn, from my face and body, replicating cuts, bruising, and blood. Truncated, burst tubes of fake blood outline me—the aftermaths of hours of stabbing, slashing, and eventual dismemberment. Plaster casts and animatronics encumber, but enliven me. The instruments of a memorable, excessive kill, scorched by bleach and salt.

I straighten and lift the curtain, unmute every track, and refill every blood tube. My axe breaks the silence and silences the critic. Only now do they realize that this is not an act.

One woman sprints into her office, but her pace slows, as she circles the perimeter of her office floor, as if disoriented in a maze. Her screams fade and quiet, as she slumps onto the prop snow and goes still, hypothermia claiming her.

A man's designer shoes pound the pavement as he flees, only for a hand to claw at his shirt collar. His eyes widen—he's not outside at all. He's at the edge of the property, tied to a tree. A gloved hand plunges a knife into him, an inch below his naval, and slits his torso open, stopping at his sternum. Our view tracks along the killer's hand and robed sleeve, as the hunting knife stabs into the side of his neck and rakes forward, slitting his jugular vein and throat from the side.

A woman, strapped to a chair, startles awake. She gapes at a reflection in her office's inset window, and the bars sprouting from the sides of the inner window frame, meeting in the middle. A police uniform and badge, encrusted with blood, flicker over her clothes. Two pieces of a rusty device, encasing her head and prying her jaws open, spring apart. The tissue in her lips and cheeks stretches and tears, the hooks in her mouth permanently ripping it open, her lower jaw thudding into her lap.

Another man, passed out on the floor, screams as he awakes, till his vocal cords give out. Gloved hands with honed fingertips drag him off the floor, out of his hiding place under his desk, and across the ceiling of his office, streaking it with blood.

One woman's eyes widen, one of her arms held rigid as if holding a gun. Bullets fired through the office doorway rip through her body, which crumples to the ground, fragments of the police uniform, designed for this moment, fluttering to the floor. The cables attached to the woman's aloft fingers slacken.

Between kills, I chop the ax downward, hinging on realist, practical effects alone: No stunt personnel, no blood tubes, no stand-ins. Skull and tooth fragments ricochet off my clear glasses, and blood gushes against my jeans and T-shirt. My clear raincoat over a dark suit superimposes over me: What they see, as the ax blade sheers chunks off of their face.

I blink to clear the viscera from my eyes and clean smudges off my glasses. I yell, "Cut!" to no one with a megaphone's force, ripping the feigned stitches binding my lips apart. I push the office door open, free from the dulled deathtrap and my supposed tomb. Employees cram both sides of the hall. Do they gawk at the room beyond me, at the portion of the set I preserved, or the illusory blood dripping from my open lip wounds, and the restored gore caking my body?

The jostling staff parts as Erick—great posture, impaled a whirling blender into his colleague's skull, taught me how to MacGyver makeup—sprints to me. I take his shoulders before he can bowl me over. "Everyone's okay," he wheezes, pointing behind him. "I've repaired almost all the damage."

His finger hovers over the remains of ragged holes in the walls, the results of managers and department heads' exploded skulls, everyone he greeted this morning. He pushes onward in his enthusiasm, taking my arm and dragging me away from the office.

My closest friends lean against the walls at the end of the hall, to either side of the elevator. Paula from accounting—designated restaurant table booker, recommender for my therapist three years ago, creator of an Excel themed drinking game—grins. She hefts a briefcase in one hand, labeled 'Murders and Acqusitions,' the edges of the tape smeared with her manager's blood. Erick guffaws at the misspelling before I can.

Paula opens it, revealing documents nestled within. The board of directors' and C suite's names, and URLs linking to digital copies of the memo and five year strategic plan, adorn the front page. Blood rushes to my head, as my eyes zoom in on the most important text: Employee ownership and Cut Above Films. I topple back, as if a weight bludgeoned my skull—like Paula bludgeoned her manager with the tape dispenser clutched in her other hand. At the same time, scars crisscross her face and scalp: Her intended narrative, of her manager inflicting the same wounds.

Erick catches me, leaning me on his shoulder. On the way down the elevator, his hands cradle me. I can't even nod in thanks. He transfers still frames of the ritual between us. Employees barred doors, placed extra lights, and observe management making their morning cups of coffee and tea. Erick and the employees confirm how many executives and team leaders lull themselves into a false sense of security, before returning to their desks.

I exit the elevator—or rather, Erick throws me out in his excitement. Gene—smart, perfect notetaker, can cut two hours of footage down to ninety faster than me—waves us over. Paula flashes the briefcase, and Gene grins. "Anything else planned today, Mr. Grace?"

I shrug. "We'll talk after Erick gets our college friends through onboarding. I have to update the content calendar first."

I jab Erick in the ribs with an elbow. "And don't call me Mr. Grace unless Erick's here."

The sarcastic remarks don't deter my friends, who follow me to my office. On first glance, only the five hundred-dollar ergonomic chair demonstrates my CEO status. At least, until Gene turns my chin toward an untouched, adjoining bathroom—toilet brushes in an open cabinet under the sink and all. A bloody hacksaw hangs on the door, slanted at the same angle Gene wielded it at as she chased the former CEO into his own bathroom and slashed his throat, even after he played dead. The flash of a jagged, oozing line across her own throat, superimposes over our group's vision, but only as I stare at the hacksaw. I gape at her.

She crosses to the bathroom door and unhooks the hacksaw. At her seat, she lays it across her knees and doesn't break eye contact. "He flayed me every day I worked for him. He didn't appreciate my life. He didn't deserve to live."

Erick lets go of me, his clenched fists shaking with repressed rage.

I grab a chair and motion for him to sit. He accepts: He's already logged into his email account. He doesn't cut away from the tears rolling down his face and obscuring his eyes, as he sends out a company-wide conference call link. Confirmation pings drown out my sobs of relief, as every participant joins it. In silence, Erick shares his screen and enters the subject line: *Cut Above Films November 2024 Company Newsletter*. As he starts the email, he beckons me to his side. Even as Paula and Gene hold me upright, they analyze Erick's email, but relax after the first sentence.

Before anything else? Thank you, a thousand times over. Thank you for everything you do, big and small. Cut Above Films wouldn't exist without each and every one of you.

We sacrifice our mental wellbeing, endanger our financial stability, and combat instant gratification, to pursue our creative passions. I empathized with every potential hire I interviewed and glimpsed these realities through their answers.

But I couldn't assuage their fears without violating company policy regarding preferential treatment toward job candidates.

I'm proud that I stuck alongside you, when my colleagues blinded themselves with their wealth and status. And I feel beyond validated that the burnout I've endured over decades in the film industry, and at Belko, Pierce, and Vernon Inc., is universal, shredding intergenerational barriers.

He can't come to the computer right now, but I know

that Errin Leslie Grace, our new CEO and president, feels the same way I do. I mentored him during the most vulnerable time in his life: His first year out of high school, and only internship he joined during the COVID-19 pandemic. I gave him the experience I would've wanted on my first splatter film set—what I wanted to give every new hire.

But now I can do that for everyone.

Take care,

Erick Allen Julian

BIOGRAPHIES

JANUARY

A PNWC and Bumbershoot award-winning poet and Seattle Times bestselling novelist, Jennifer DiMarco first toured nationally as an author when she was nineteen years old, having written novels since the age of ten. The first sixteen years of her career included the publication of contemporary drama, high fantasy, science fiction, poetry, and mystery novels as well as the production of two short films and three stage plays. During a twenty-year hiatus from prose, DiMarco married, raised two children, and worked as a filmmaker writing and directing more than a dozen feature films, half a dozen mini series, and more than a hundred short films. She returned to prose with *Hannah at Night and Twelve Other Stories* in 2020. DiMarco lives in the Pacific Northwest with her wife, composer and actor Brianne, and their adult children, author and illustrator Maxwell, and actor and illustrator Faith.

FEBRUARY

Joe Nasta is the author of four books of poetry and the fiction collection *Halve It* (Blue Forge Press, 2025). Ze is an associate editor for Elizabeth Ellen's Hobart, a multimedia artist and writer, & a foodie in Seattle. Find him online as @roflcoptermcgee or adventuring with his dog Alacrán.

MARCH

Gregor Fjellrev is an author, musician, actor, martial artist, woodworker, strategy game enthusiast and black hole of carbonated, fermented, and distilled beverages alike from Auburn, Washington. His winner for 2025 *Compliment of the Year* was, while participating in the 'No Kings' Protest in his hometown, after having stood in the beating sun for two full hours after everyone else had gotten bored and left, a person approached and said that 'we need more people like you' in recognition of his stalwartness.

Fjellrev's other published writing includes the *Universal Defender* series of both novella and novel-length works as well as other books available at www.BlueForgePress.com. Find his albums at www.BlueForgeRecords.com

APRIL

Michelle Lee is a Pacific Northwest native with an imagination open to possibilities. In her downtime, Michelle is an avid reader, loves to explore different areas in the northwest, speaks fluent sarcasm, and loves baking bread. She loves to hear from readers and can be found on Facebook and Instagram.

MAY

Bree Indigo is a poet and songwriter. She enjoys tarot, exploring Washington State's Olympic Peninsula, and tending to her menagerie of pets. She has been published in all volumes of *Unnerving* and all volumes of the women's poetry and essay collection, *Rise*. Indigo lives with her wife and their family in the Puget Sound. Find her on Instagram @bree_indigo

JUNE

Nathan Sykes is the author of *Snowfall's Embrace & Other Graveyard Sagas from Beyond the Sister Moons*, a collection of tales that blur the boundary between the familiar and the strange. A writer from a young age, he draws inspiration from the stories that influenced him the most growing up. He has an enduring fascination with possibility, and a love for questions that have no answers. When he isn't writing, Nathan enjoys live music and wandering in nature. He lives in Edgewood, Washington, with his children and two cats.

JULY

Hailing from Tacoma, WA, Lauren Patzer has been an information technology guru, actor, writer and film producer among other pursuits. His love of horror began with a non-stop reading of *The Amityville Horror*. With two novels and over fifty short stories published now, his most recent work is the horror novel *Undead Reckoning*.

AUGUST

From reading children's books to grade school students, to creating the Senior to Senior Intergenerational Communications project, J.W. Capek has always appreciated the art of storytelling! Growing up in Arizona, teaching high school and raising a family in California, J.W. moved to the Northwest to be an author. Her *Deerwhere Codex* trilogy creates a world with quantum computers, epigenetics, and three unique genders. J.W.'s short stories span the human experience from tragedy to ridiculous. Read more of them in *Fragments of Time* and look for *Facets of a Crystal Mind* this winter, both available from Blue Forge Press. Check out www.jwcapek.com for current information.

SEPTEMBER

Author, illustrator, and award-winning actor and filmmaker, Maxwell DiMarco has been writing professionally since he was a child. DiMarco lives in the Pacific Northwest, where he works as a special effects editor and is the host of the weekly children's series, Seriously Cereal. He has also written for every volume of Unnerving, where he explores the darker aspects of society through physical and psychological horror. He is a huge believer in community, acceptance, and seeing the world from all perspectives, striving to always provide his readers with an intriguing, thought-provoking narrative, no matter the genre.

OCTOBER

Marshall Miller retired from Homeland Security and police enforcement to more deeply explore the human condition and what drives us as a species. Framed with the arrival of alien Apex predators who see us as little more than a food source, Miller is best known for crafting his series, *The Tschaaa Infestation*, that dares to ask: Are we truly superior and do we deserve to survive? Creatures, beasties, and strong female characters feature often in Marshall Miller's Tschaaa Infestation and his Special Agent Kim Kupar series. Find out more about his work at www.tiny.cc/marshallmiller

NOVEMBER

Marvin Vialle, a longtime resident of Tacoma,Washington, was born and raised on a small farm in rural Kansas. After college, Marvin moved to Washington State where he served for several decades as an environmental planner and manager for the state's Department of Ecology. Upon retirement, he turned his attention to writing children's books and short stories, and currently, he's working on a novel. Marvin also spends a lot of time attending his grandsons' sports events.

DECEMBER

Amber Rainey is a writer with a passion for storytelling that blends heart, creativity, and authenticity. With a background in technology as a systems analyst, she brings a unique perspective to her work—infusing every project with both analytical insight and an eye for human connection. Amber believes stories have the power to inspire change, spark imagination, and bring people together. When she isn't writing, you can find her enjoying quiet moments with her family and cats, exploring new creative outlets, and connecting with her community.

THIRTEEN

Pauline Ugalde is a visually-impaired writer, gamer, and metalhead. Her favorite genres are sci-fi, fantasy, and horror. She learned metanarrative structure from Toby Fox, and how to write compelling characters from Tobin Bell.

Robert Eggers hammered home that research could elevate her stories. She began celebrating her chosen fandoms, by following the examples modeled by James A. Janisse and Chelsea Rebecca. Her favorite scary movie is *Saw X*.

www.ingramcontent.com/pod-product-compliance
Lightning Source LLC
Chambersburg PA
CBHW060410310726

48976CB00003B/1003